# Praise for Johnny Townsend

In *Zombies for Jesus*, "Townsend isn't writing satire, but deeply emotional and revealing portraits of people who are, with a few exceptions, quite lovable."

Kel Munger, *Sacramento News and Review*

Townsend's stories are "a gay *Portnoy's Complaint* of Mormonism. Salacious, sweet, sad, insightful, insulting, religiously ethnic, quirky-faithful, and funny."

D. Michael Quinn, author of *The Mormon Hierarchy: Origins of Power*

Johnny Townsend is "an important voice in the Mormon community."

Stephen Carter, editor of *Sunstone* magazine

"Told from a believably conversational first-person perspective, [*The Abominable Gayman*'s] novelistic focus on Anderson's journey to thoughtful self-acceptance allows for greater character development than often seen in short stories, which makes this well-paced work rich and satisfying, and one of Townsend's strongest. An extremely important contribution to the field of Mormon fiction." Named to Kirkus Reviews' Best of 2011.

Kirkus Reviews

"The Buzzard Tree," from *The Circumcision of God*, was listed as a finalist for the 2007 Whitney Award for Best Short LDS Fiction.

"The Rift," from *The Abominable Gayman*, is a "fascinating tale of an untenable situation...a *tour de force*."

David Lenson, editor, *The Massachusetts Review*

"Pronouncing the Apostrophe," from *The Golem of Rabbi Loew*, is "quiet and revealing, an intriguing tale..."

Sima Rabinowitz, Literary Magazine Review, NewPages.com

"Johnny Townsend's short stories cannot be pigeon-holed. His keen observations on the human condition come in many shapes and sizes...reflecting on both his Jewish and Mormon backgrounds as well as life in the vast and varied American gay community. He dares to think and write about people and incidents that frighten away more timid artists. His perspective is sometimes startling, sometimes hilarious, sometimes poignant, but always compassionate."

Gerald S. Argetsinger, Artistic Director of the Hill Cumorah Pageant (1990-96)

*The Circumcision of God* is "a collection of short stories that consider the imperfect, silenced majority of Mormons, who may in fact be [the Church's] best hope....[The book leaves] readers regretting the church's willingness to marginalize those who best exemplify its ideals: those who love fiercely despite all obstacles, who brave challenges at great personal risk and who always choose the hard, higher road."

Kirkus Reviews

In *Mormon Fairy Tales*, Johnny Townsend displays "both a wicked sense of irony and a deep well of compassion."

Kel Munger, *Sacramento News and Review*

"*Selling the City of Enoch* exists at that awkward intersection where the LDS ideal meets the real world, and Townsend navigates his terrain with humor, insight, and pathos."

Donna Banta, author of *False Prophet*

*The Golem of Rabbi Loew* will prompt "gasps of outrage from conservative readers...a strong collection."

Kirkus Reviews

"That's one of the reasons why I found Johnny Townsend's new book *Mormon Fairy Tales* SO MUCH FUN!! Without fretting about what the theology is supposed to be if it were pinned down, Townsend takes you on a voyage to explore the rich-but-undertapped imagination of Mormonism. I loved his portrait of spirit prison! He really nailed it—not in an official doctrine sort of way, but in a sort of 'if you know Mormonism, you know this is what it must be like' way—and what a prison it is!

Johnny Townsend has written at least ten books of Mormon stories. So far, I've read only two (*Mormon Fairy Tales* and *The Circumcision of God*), but I'm planning to read the rest—and you should too, if you'd like a fun and interesting new perspective on Mormons in life and imagination!"

C. L. Hanson, *Main Street Plaza*

*Zombies for Jesus* is "eerie, erotic, and magical."

Publishers Weekly

"While [Townsend's] many touching vignettes draw deeply from Mormon mythology, history, spirituality and culture, [*Mormon Fairy Tales*] is neither a gaudy act of proselytism nor angry protest literature from an ex-believer. Like all good fiction, his stories are simply about the joys, the hopes and the sorrows of people."

Kirkus Reviews

"In *Let the Faggots Burn* author Johnny Townsend restores this tragic event [the UpStairs Lounge fire] to its proper place in

LGBT history and reminds us that the victims of the blaze were not just 'statistics,' but real people with real lives, families, and friends."

Jesse Monteagudo, The Bilerico Project

*Marginal Mormons* is "an irreverent, honest look at life outside the mainstream Mormon Church....Throughout his musings on sin and forgiveness, Townsend beautifully demonstrates his characters' internal, perhaps irreconcilable struggles....Rather than anger and disdain, he offers an honest portrayal of people searching for meaning and community in their lives, regardless of their life choices or secrets." Named to Kirkus Reviews' Best of 2012.

Kirkus Reviews

"The Sneakover Prince" from *God's Gargoyles* is "one of the most sweet and romantic stor[ies] I have ever read."

Elisa Rolle, Reviews and Ramblings, founder of The Rainbow Awards

"*Let the Faggots Burn* is a one-of-a-kind piece of history. Without Townsend's diligence and devotion, many details would've been lost forever. With his tremendous foresight and tenacious research, Townsend put a face on this tragedy at a time when few people would talk about it....Through Townsend's vivid writing, you will sense what it must've been like in those final moments as the fire ripped through the

UpStairs Lounge. *Let the Faggots Burn* is a chilling and insightful glimpse into a largely forgotten and ignored chapter of LGBT history."

Robert Camina, writer and producer of the documentary
*Raid of the Rainbow Lounge*

The stories in *The Mormon Victorian Society* "register the new openness and confidence of gay life in the age of same-sex marriage....What hasn't changed is Townsend's wry, conversational prose, his subtle evocations of character and social dynamics, and his deadpan humor. His warm empathy still glows in this intimate yet clear-eyed engagement with Mormon theology and folkways. Funny, shrewd and finely wrought dissections of the awkward contradictions—and surprising harmonies—between conscience and desire." Named to Kirkus Reviews' Best of 2013.

Kirkus Reviews

"Johnny Townsend's 'Partying with St. Roch' [in the anthology *Latter-Gay Saints*] tells a beautiful, haunting tale."

Kent Brintnall, Out in Print: Queer Book Reviews

"The struggles and solutions of the individuals [in *Latter-Gay Saints*] will resonate across faith traditions and help readers better understand the cost of excluding gay members from full religious participation."

Publishers Weekly

"Mormon Movie Marathon," from *Selling the City of Enoch*, "is funny, constructively critical, but also sad because the desire...for belonging is so palpable."

Levi S. Peterson, author of *The Backslider* and *The Canyons of Grace*

*Selling the City of Enoch* is "sharply intelligent...pleasingly complex...The stories are full of...doubters, but there's no vindictiveness in these pages; the characters continuously poke holes in Mormonism's more extravagant absurdities, but they take very little pleasure in doing so....Many of Townsend's stories...have a provocative edge to them, but this [book] displays a great deal of insight as well...a playful, biting and surprisingly warm collection."

Kirkus Reviews

# Behind the Zion Curtain

Johnny Townsend

BookLocker.com, Inc.
2014

First Edition

Cover design by Todd Engel

Dedicated to Gary Tolman,
who astonishes me every day
with his goodness

Special thanks to Donna Banta
for her editorial assistance

# Contents

Introduction: Drinking the Kool-Aid ............... xix

Fire in an Empty Pool ........................................ 1

Burying My Baby at Deseret Land and Livestock .......................... 10

Gardening without Deet ........................... 29

Vitamin-Rich Baptisms for the Dead ................. 37

Equity for Monica ................................ 46

Lyeing for the Lord ................................ 55

A Tithing of Queers ................................ 64

The Entomology of Words ........................... 77

Trapped in a Vagina ................................ 86

Till Death Do Us Part ................................ 97

An Endowed Spy ................................ 109

The Girl Next Store ................................ 119

Star Fleet Testing ................................ 127

My Path to the Gutter ................................ 139

The God of Macramé ................................ 150

The Neurochemistry of Monday Night ................ 157

Group Sex for Faithful Mormons ................... 165

The Bishop's Husband ................................ 174

Also by Johnny Townsend ........................... 185

# Introduction:
# Drinking the Kool-Aid

I've heard some ex-Mormons say, "The Church isn't like it used to be forty years ago. It's changed. It's gotten worse. I loved the Church when I was young. But it's gotten so mean-spirited these days."

In some ways, I share that feeling. But when I think back more carefully, I'm not at all sure it's true. When the first black members began joining my suburban New Orleans ward, I still heard the N-word bandied about by several congregants. Around the same time, when the Equal Rights Amendment was coming up for a vote, we were told by the Church to rally against it. We didn't have to understand the particulars. The Church told us to oppose it so we opposed it. Thousands of us showed up in Baton Rouge to show that "good, God-fearing people" were against such an abominable amendment. An amendment which simply guaranteed that women weren't treated perpetually as second-class citizens.

That seems pretty mean-spirited to me.

In 1978, when Jim Jones murdered 913 of his followers in Jonestown, Latter-day Saints shook their heads and pitied the poor souls who would so easily follow a "false prophet." *They'd* never follow someone so blindly and ignorantly.

And yet how many LDS families have turned their backs on the gay and lesbian members of their families who have come out, even to the point of driving their teenage children to homelessness or suicide? These homosexual sinners, the families feel, have given up their slot in the Celestial Kingdom, so there is obviously no reason to have anything more to do with them.

This from a Church that says family is the most important thing not only in this world but also in the eternities. Just chuck aside anyone who is different. If our own flesh and blood lies dying in a gutter, that's no concern of ours.

But it's not only a matter of callous indifference. How many stalwart members sacrificed tens of thousands of dollars from their children's college education funds or their own retirement funds to donate to the Prop 8 campaign in California, solely to keep loving couples from marrying? In the temple, we commit that when asked we will give up all our possessions to further the Lord's work, so because Church leaders said in 2008 that giving up our life's savings was the right thing to do to keep those miserable gays in their place, now good Mormon children will grow up without the opportunity to go to college. Elderly couples will live on the edge of poverty.

Who says we haven't drunk the Kool-Aid?

The Mormon ideal is to one day live the United Order. We idolize the people of the City of Enoch for living "with all things in common." We revere the Nephites and Lamanites after Christ's visit to America who lived in complete peace because they had "neither rich nor poor among them." In modern political terminology, this would clearly be called Socialism. But say that word to a Mormon today, and he or she will have an apoplectic fit.

Is it apostasy to want to emulate the lifestyle of the City of Enoch, a city so righteous that it was taken up into heaven?

Mormons are so afraid of apostasy that they shun any former members who have been excommunicated in order to avoid contaminating themselves. They think that because they are members of the "one, true church" that as a group they are immune from apostasy. Individual "bad" people can go astray, but not the Church as a whole. And maybe the Church "as a whole" won't. Over the last several years, however, I've watched as more and more Church members have subconsciously converted to another religion, which is pretty much the definition of apostasy. Now the bulk of American Latter-day Saints are more Republican than they are Mormon.

Robert Gehrke in the *Salt Lake Tribune* points out that in the past few decades "Mormon voters have become more and more ensconced in the Republican Party, to the point that today they represent the most reliable, cohesive bloc of voters for the GOP of nearly any demographic" ("Mormons' close-knit nature, values drive them to GOP," 15 Sept 2014). In his article, Gehrke discusses the book, *Seeking the Promised Land*, by David Campbell, John C. Green, and Quin Monson and concludes that "the three authors warn that having the church linked too closely with the Republican Party could undermine church interests."

I'm afraid it's too late for that.

Mormons used to care about the poor, but Republicans say that the poor are poor because they don't work hard enough, and more Mormons believe this every day, and vote for politicians who won't help the poor. For a religion that believes in welfare for its own, it's ironic that it doesn't believe in welfare for others. But that is what the Republican religion preaches from the pulpit, so that is the attitude they adopt. As members of the Republican religion, they support those policies which benefit almost solely the top 1%. They have fallen away from traditional Mormon beliefs.

There is no scriptural support for Capitalism in either the Bible or the Book of Mormon, yet Mormons believe that Capitalism was created by God, because that is what their new religion, the Republican Party, teaches them. Traditional Mormon doctrine never taught them that.

They are drinking *someone's* Kool-Aid. But whose?

Mormons used to believe that the government didn't have the right to tell them what kind of marriages they could have, but now as Republicans they believe that there should be laws banning the types of marriages *they* don't like.

Mormons used to believe in exercising stewardship over the land, but because Republicans support Big Oil and eliminating any regulations that diminish pollution, they support these measures, too. They don't just do these things as political acts; they believe they are literally following God's will when they follow Republican policies. As if supporting wind energy or wave energy or solar energy, energies provided by God, would somehow be an unforgiveable sin.

Katherine Hayhoe, the climate scientist who is also an evangelical Christian and whose husband is a pastor, says basically the same thing about evangelicals. There is nothing inherent in Christianity which prevents believers from accepting the reality of climate change and committing themselves to doing something about it, except that there have been no significant Christian leaders in the past few decades, so people have ended up following Republican leaders instead. As a result, evangelicals now feel it is a sin to believe scientists on this issue, when there is just as much proof behind climate change as there is behind diabetes research, and yet few Christians feel it is a sin to use insulin, just because insulin was recommended by scientists. Hayhoe is optimistic that she can convince a hundred million American evangelical Christians that not only is it okay to work to reverse climate change, but also that God actually expects it of us morally. The fact that 99% of the hate mail and death threats she receives come from faithful Christians shows that she has a hard road ahead of her. Brigham Young taught that "our religion will not clash with nor contradict the facts of science in any particular," yet since the Republican religion teaches that there is no truth to climate change, Mormons believe it. We are basically in the same boat as evangelicals on this one.

In fact, it often seems we are becoming more and more like evangelicals on many issues. We used to pride ourselves on being a "peculiar" people, but now we want to be just like all the other fundamentalists, to show them we're on the same team. It's because our Republican "prophets" are telling both us and evangelicals the same thing. If Mormons weren't apostatizing by putting more faith in Republican politics than traditional LDS doctrine, they're certainly doing it by trying to blend in more with other Christian sects rather than boldly standing out as the "one and only true church."

Mormons used to care about fiscal responsibility, but now they support politicians who gleefully threaten to send the U.S. into default and possibly trigger a global Depression. They believe, both as Mormons and as Republicans, in the apocalypse that will occur just before the Second Coming. However, what they fail to remember, no longer being true Mormons, is that the bad times are supposed to come about because of *evil* people, not because of God's followers. Now *they* are the ones trying to *create* those bad times.

Mormons used to believe that the president of the LDS Church and the Twelve Apostles were "prophets, seers, and revelators," but now they believe that Glenn Beck, Sean Hannity, Ted Cruz, and Bill O'Reilly are the true prophets. Apostate Mormons watch Fox News religiously (and I *mean* religiously) and refuse to watch other, "godless" stations. To members of the Republican religion, watching MSNBC is like asking a Mormon to attend Baptist services or, God forbid, a Catholic mass. So these former Mormons go where the news is altered to accommodate their new religious beliefs, kind of like the Joseph Smith translation of the King James Version of the Bible. Information is edited to support their points. To Mormons, Fox News is gospel.

I know it sounds harsh to call millions of temple-recommend-holding Mormons apostates. But this is not an exaggeration. This is not a metaphor. The fact is that millions of Mormons have been led to depart from the original teachings of the Church. So it seems the Church really *has* changed in the last forty years.

I'm not stating all this because I'm particularly concerned about the purity of the Church. And change in itself is not a bad thing. In fact, I wish the Church would change some more. I just feel it needs to be said because, for all his other failings, Joseph Smith did have *some* things right. If we're going to change, let's change the bad things, not the good things.

For better or for worse, Mormons are followers, not independent thinkers. So when people they believe speak for God tell them what to do and what to believe, they do it and they believe it. And to them, God's mouthpiece is the Republican leader of the day.

Th
war
who
Be

Johnny Townsend

from the Republican faith if they ever d
back then, Mormons followed
Republican teachings, and agreed w
Readers most likely still t
based on my own political
Gallup poll from July 2014
by faith, Mormons had th
out of members of all re
I don't call Mor
belong to a partic
Mormon Democ
to name-callin
because their
directs ho
church l
religion
those
led

thos

For its first c.
maintain a reasonably
past couple of decades, faithfu.
worthiness of Mormon Democ..
Mormonism taught them that Democrats .
because that is what their new religion, the Repu.
taught them. When Republicans were just a political part,
not a religion, Mormon Democrats weren't demonized as they
are now. We even had Democrat apostles. But the Republican
Party is now a religion for most Mormons, one they follow at
all costs, no matter who gets hurt, because that's what the
Republican political leaders whom they believe speak for God
teach them that God wants.

Mormons today don't mention the fact that the state of Utah
voted overwhelmingly for Franklin Delano Roosevelt in 1932.
And 1936. And 1940. And 1944. The members of the
Republican religion in Utah today would be excommunicated

...d such a thing now. But ...Mormon teachings, not ...ith FDR's principles.

...hink I'm overstating the case ...eliefs. But did anyone see that ...which showed that when compared ...e lowest opinion of President Obama ...gions? Coincidence?

...mon Republicans apostates because they ...lar political party, the way they determine ...ats are apostates. And I'm not trying to resort ...g. I mean this literally. I call them apostates ...affiliation to their political party overwhelmingly ...y they construct policies and doctrines for their ...ves just as much as for their secular lives. The two ...s have become so fully intertwined and conflated that ...members of the Church don't even realize they've been ...astray. It's like the "boiling frog syndrome." The change ...curred so slowly that everyone adapted as they went along, ...nd now they're fully followers of the Republican religion and don't even realize they are Mormons in name only. Especially since they are so proud to be Mormons. It would be ironic if it weren't so sad.

The scriptures teach us that no man can serve two masters. Mormons are torn between being true to Mormonism and being true to the Republican Party. Unfortunately for the Mormon Church, the Republican Party is easily the winning contestant in this battle. Being Republican and supporting Republican values is clearly more important to most Mormons now than following traditional Mormon teachings. It is quite obviously more important than being good citizens and caring for their fellow man.

The leaders of the Mormon Church should be concerned that they are losing their members to a usurper. But then, most of them have secretly converted to the Republican religion as well.

I don't deny that the vast majority of Mormons are good, decent people. They most certainly are. Just as the followers of Jim Jones were.

Christ healed the sick without asking for payment. Caring for the sick without expecting compensation used to be considered a "Christian" act. In fact, a very large number of missionaries from other religions are actually medical missionaries. But we as Mormons call the idea of universal healthcare "death panels." Is providing healthcare for all people really something we think Christ would oppose? Caring for the sick is bad? Caring for the poor means we're being led astray? Helping those suffering is a sin?

Doesn't Isaiah warn the faithful not to call evil good and good evil?

Mormons have no problem telling me to my face that I'm going to hell. And yet I know they'll be terribly offended by the blunt things I've just said. The funny thing is that I really don't mean to say anything inflammatory. And yet the Jason Chaffetzes and Gail Ruzickas of Mormondom would have me banned from every library and bookstore, if not arrested outright, simply for stating what should be obvious to anyone.

I'm afraid I risk my reputation, what little there is, as a fiction writer by writing an essay like this. I remember as a teenager reading a dozen or so books by Robert A. Heinlein. I loved him and couldn't get enough. Until I read one of his essays and realized his actual feelings about politics. I could never read his work again without seeing the writer behind the writing. It was a loss for me.

But some things need to be said plainly and clearly. The Mormon Church is at risk of losing its soul. Whether its soul is something worth saving is another matter, of course. But I personally think it is. I'd like to encourage the LDS to realize that suicide drills won't always remain drills.

Oh, I just heard some Mormons ranting against workers' unions and treating employees fairly.

Kool-Aid, anyone?

# Fire in an Empty Pool

"The pool's finally empty, honey," said my husband, Dean, over breakfast. "We can start demolishing it in a few days."

I put another slice of turkey bacon on his plate. "I can't wait," I replied. "That thing has always been more trouble than it's worth."

"You just wait, Meredith," Dean said, grinning. "When we buy our next house, you'll insist on another pool."

"Who wants to move?" I replied. "I just moved in here three months ago." We'd be getting married in another month. Life was idyllic with my dream doctor boyfriend.

He laughed. "People always get tired of the status quo and want to move on," he said.

I thought of the girl he dumped to start dating me.

"Just like you did with your church," he added.

I groaned. Why did he have to mention that? I'd been a True Believer, like everyone else in my family, until about a year ago, when I'd stumbled upon an ex-Mormon website and started learning things I'd never known before. I still believed that probably half of the "real truths" about Mormonism were exaggerated or downright lies, but with even just a handful of them verifiable, I found I had to rethink my membership in the Church. While I still hadn't officially resigned or been excommunicated, now that I was "living in sin," it could happen any day, especially with my stalwart sister Ellen checking up on my morality every day.

"Yes, but I'm not moving on to a *new* religion," I pointed out. "Just no religion at all. Following your analogy, that would make us homeless."

"You'll find something to replace it with. Something bigger and better." Dean scooped the last of his scrambled egg onto his fork. "Just like this place. I'm only thirty-two. After a few years when I have some real money, you may want a larger house."

I laughed. "I'm twenty-four, and this house has five bedrooms. How many kids do you think I plan to have?"

"All right, Meredith, all right," said Dean, still grinning in a slightly condescending fashion. "We'll grow old here together." He paused. "With our six kids."

He went to brush his teeth, and I started cleaning the table. Funny how after escaping traditional Mormonism, I still ended up a housewife, even with my degree in journalism. But I did have an active blog, Gothic Ex-Mormon, followed by almost 350 people.

I shook my head. I was hardly going to change the world, was I?

After Dean left for the clinic, I walked about the house, feeling a sense of uneasy anticipation. Almost everything in the house belonged to Dean, and I wanted to make it more "our" place than me just living in his. My insisting on removing the pool was one of those attempts. I had a photo of myself in my typical goth outfit, inside a gargoyle frame, on the mantelpiece, but all the other photos of my family members just reminded me again of Mormonism. There was Ellen and her husband in front of the Salt Lake temple. There was my brother and his wife in front of the Los Angeles temple. My oldest sister and her husband in front of the Mesa temple. And there were my mother and father in front of the San Diego temple. Even the photos of the kids were taken with a portrait of the First Presidency looming in the background. One horrific family photo of my parents, my three siblings and I, and the available grandkids at the time, had us all dressed in white, as if we'd passed on to the other side and were now happily living our afterlife in heaven.

Dad's white jumpsuit suggested that apparently there were still zippers in heaven.

I'd left the Church, but I hadn't left my family. Yet when they were conflated like this, sometimes I didn't know exactly where I did stand with either my family *or* the Church.

Maybe I'd request another family portrait, perhaps pay for it myself, and insist it be taken in street clothes. Despite marriages in far-off temples, we did all still live in the greater Los Angeles area. In fact, my sister Ellen lived less than half a mile from us. She'd be over here soon, visiting two or three times a week. Her visits were more like missionary work than acts of sisterly love, as she tried to bring me back into the fold. Some evening, I wanted to invite her over to watch me dancing in the back yard. Ellen had always hated the song, "Dancing in the Moonlight" by King Harvest, saying it talked of pagan, if not Satanic, rituals.

I loved dancing in the moonlight.

There was a knock on the door. I checked to make sure my spike cuff earrings were in place, and I headed for the kitchen. "Ellen!" I said as if surprised. "It's so good to see you!"

"Meredith, you're looking better every day," said my sister, looking nervously at my ears. "I'm sure once you're married, you'll have a real glow about you."

Once I was no longer fornicating, I completed Ellen's thought.

I ushered Ellen inside and offered her some lemonade. She told me about how she'd lost her car keys this morning, but got down on her knees and prayed, and lo and behold, they showed up on her coffee table. I tried not to roll my eyes, wondering if I should ask if it were against the Word of Wisdom to own a coffee table in the first place.

Next, Ellen told me about the talk she'd given at church last weekend, on the importance of avoiding liquor. "You'll never become an alcoholic if you don't take that first drink," she repeated for me. Then she shook her head and wiped at her eyes. "And you met Dean in a *bar*," she said sadly. "*Do* be careful, Meredith."

Ellen was twenty-eight, I mused, and already 180 pounds. There were other things one could become addicted to besides alcohol.

The conversation continued another thirty minutes, all the focus on Ellen, her two young children, and church activities, with no questions about Dean or myself. But things were finally winding down when Ellen did actually ask a question about me. "Do you still have your temple clothes?" she queried innocently.

I frowned. Actually, I did have them, though I didn't know why I hadn't tossed them ages ago. It irritated me to have to say yes. I felt as if she'd caught me in a lie.

"Excellent!" Ellen clapped her hands.

"Why?"

"I have a friend, Susan. She's looking after the kids right now. She's about your size. She converted almost two years ago and has never been to the temple, but she has her recommend now."

"Bully for her." My stake president had always refused my requests for one.

"I was thinking she could use your temple clothes."

I shrugged. "I don't see why not. I have the white dress, those slippers, the green apron, the robe and sash, the cap with the veil, and that pouch you can put all the accessories in."

"Wonderful! Wonderful!"

"They've never been worn," I said. I had certainly always planned to attend the temple, but I'd left the Church before I ever got permission to go. A pity, really, as it probably would have been interesting to see if all the rumors were true. "They're all in pristine shape."

"Fantastic."

I excused myself and went upstairs to my dresser. I knew exactly where the clothes were and pulled them out of the bottom drawer. Maybe it was time to cut these last few ties to the Church, anyway. Perhaps the next time I visited my parents,

I could mention that new family portrait. I carried the clothes back down the stairs.

Ellen looked through them carefully, probably making sure I hadn't embroidered any pentagrams on them. Then she started to gather them up as if about to leave.

"The dress cost me $98," I said. "And the rest of the items cost about $60 altogether. I'm happy to sell the whole lot to Susan for half what I paid. Just $80."

Ellen's mouth fell open. "You can't be serious," she breathed.

"What do you mean?"

"You can't *sell* temple clothing. It's sacrilegious."

"Well, the Church sold them to me," I pointed out.

"That's different."

"How so?"

"You just can't sell them, that's all. You have to give them away."

"I'll give them to Goodwill if I want to give them away."

Ellen gasped.

"It's $80 if she wants the clothes," I repeated.

"But Meredith, it's like Esau selling his birthright."

I took a deep breath. Was I past the emotional extortion and blackmail that I used to live with every day, I wondered? It was like trying to polish the crevices in an intricate tea platter. Mom had one, though she never served tea. Every year, the girls would have to polish till our fingers were raw. But there was always some residual tarnish left in the details. "I'll give Susan till Saturday to make up her mind."

"And then what?"

"Then they go in the trash. You're right that I need to get rid of them."

"But you won't make any money by throwing them away. If you're willing to take nothing to give them to the trash can, why can't you take nothing to give them to a person?"

I smiled. "Oh, you know how us apostates are." I pulled the clothing back over toward me.

I ushered Ellen to the door, and she left with a concerned and confused expression on her face. I looked down at the temple clothing and thought about the new dragon end table I could almost afford if I sold the clothing. I needed more of my own furniture in the house. Dean had complained at first about the one dragon mirror I'd added to the decor, but he promised he'd eventually get used to my style.

It was Thursday now, and I felt I was giving Susan ample time to make a decision. If Susan was poor, Ellen certainly had enough money to help her out. I put the clothing back in the dresser and started vacuuming the living room.

I was a damn housewife.

Maybe I should go back to school part-time and continue my education. Wouldn't hurt to get another degree or two. At least I'd be able to develop a secular self-esteem. I wasn't going to get any Mormon self-esteem out of baking brownies.

I roasted a chicken for tonight's supper. Dean loved roasted chicken.

After dinner, we went in the bedroom and did the three perverted things we'd done the night we met. I *looked* goth. He *was*. Sometimes, he hurt me a little bit, but I knew it was all his way of showing love.

Saturday afternoon, Dean and I were sitting on the sofa watching *Secrets of the Metropolitan Museum.* "I hired someone to come out on Monday morning and dig up the pool," said Dean. "It's your last chance to change your mind."

"I'll plant a vegetable garden there," I replied. "Get some fresh tomatoes and basil."

"Okay, honey."

My cell phone rang and I reached over to pick it up. "Hi, Ellen," I said.

"Susan will pay $50 and not a penny more."

I frowned. I was bullied the entire time I was in the Church. Was that simply a part of the culture? But was $30 really that big of a deal? Maybe I should at least get some money out of this. I looked at my ring which sported bat wings.

No. I wasn't going to be bullied any more. "Tell her to get an LDS account and buy them online." I hung up.

Mormonism was behind me. I'd have to change the name of my blog. Start a new chapter in my life.

Maybe I'd take an embroidery class at the community college and actually start sewing pentagrams on some of my clothing, or perhaps gothic crosses.

After a nice dinner of homemade lasagna and an episode of *Orange is the New Black*, I asked Dean to get out the video camera. I put on my sheerest goth dress and set up my portable CD player. I gathered several small branches into a pile at the bottom of the empty swimming pool and set them on fire with the help of some lighter fluid. Then, while dancing to King Harvest, I dropped my temple clothes on the flames one at a time, waving my arms in the air as I circled the pool underneath the almost full moon.

# Burying My Baby at Deseret Land and Livestock

The last time my stake hosted a Mormon Handcart reenactment, I was fourteen and just getting over a sprained ankle from my gymnastics class, so I hadn't participated. Now I was seventeen, old for a Laurel, soon to become a much anticipated Single Adult. I still wasn't sure the Trek sounded all that exciting, but the bishop and stake president and Laurel president were all pushing the three-day adventure quite hard.

"You'll get to experience what our ancestors did," my Mom pointed out again this evening over dinner.

"The Jews don't celebrate their slavery in Egypt by becoming slaves for three days," I said. "They have a great meal while reclining."

"You can't have empathy unless you truly understand what our forefathers and mothers went through." said Dad.

"Do I need to be tarred and feathered to appreciate Joseph Smith?"

"Now, Melanie, be nice."

I finished my dinner and went upstairs. I didn't even have chores like dishwashing, I realized, lying on my bed. Maybe I truly was a little spoiled living in the 21$^{st}$ century. Perhaps three days pushing a handcart in northern Utah wouldn't be too detrimental to my emotional health. Still, we wouldn't be allowed to bring our cell phones, so there'd be no texting for three days. What were we, Neanderthals?

I'd already had to sew a period dress that I'd be wearing. But at least they'd let us bring our tennis shoes. I called my best friend, Jen.

"What do you think?" I asked. "Are you going?"

"My parents said I'd be grounded for three whole weeks if I didn't."

"I love the subtle way gospel principles are taught." I laughed but Jen did not.

"Three days spending the night in sleeping bags with ticks everywhere?" she asked. "Three days of porta-potties?"

"Just look at it as training for when you go to BYU," I said.

"What do you mean?" Both Jen and I planned to go to Brigham Young University next year.

"They have a Study Abroad course where you get to walk the entire 1400 mile trek the pioneers used on the Mormon Trail."

"Oh, my heck. Don't tell my parents that!"

We talked about the cute non-member boy who sometimes attended Sunday school named David, and about mean Brother Sidney who taught the class, and then after making fun of Sister Patterson, the teacher for the MIA Maids, we hung up.

My parents were making me pay the $15 participation fee for the Trek out of my allowance. Talk about suffering for my faith.

So on Thursday morning, Mom dropped me off at church, and I sat next to Jen as our Laurel president drove us and a couple of younger girls to Woodruff. There were about fifteen to twenty kids from each ward, and nine wards in the stake, so there'd be about 180 teens participating, plus a few adult chaperones. I'd be wearing this same yellow dress for three days, but I had a small pack with extra underwear and socks. And a few Almond Joy bars I'd smuggled with me.

Jen leaned over and whispered, "I've got six granola bars if you ever get desperate out there, Melanie."

Granola sounded too much like what the pioneers might have eaten.

We arrived at Deseret Land and Livestock still early in the morning, a huge Church farm that promised twenty-five miles of ranch roads and cross country walking. "All right," said a man after everybody was out of the cars and vans and standing in a huge crowd, "this is Brother and Sister Clawson. They're a missionary couple and will go with you on the Trek. They'll be able to tell you pioneer stories at night after dinner. And here are Tom Bradley and Derek Peters. They're two recreation students. They'll be assisting you along the way."

Jen nudged me and nodded toward Derek.

"We'll be providing a water trailer and the porta-john trailer, and of course the handcarts, but your stake leaders will be providing the food. You'll have some with you on the Trek, but someone will be driving to appointed meeting places to bring the suppers." He smiled broadly. "So you see, it won't be as bad as some of you have imagined."

"Where's the trailer carrying the Xboxes?" shouted a boy in back of the crowd. Everyone laughed.

"You'll find it a relief to be away from modern civilization for a few days," said the man. "In fact, you may find that you actually want to turn off the computer when you get back home. Many of—"

"What if I get a blister?" shouted another boy. More laughter.

"We have Sister Gunderson with us," announced a man from one of the other wards. "She's a registered nurse."

The introductory pep talk continued a few more minutes. We would be at an elevation between 6500 and 7500 feet for the next three days. The area consisted of rolling hills covered in prairie grass and sage, with some small canyons here and there. As residents of Utah, we already knew how to watch out for snakes and scorpions. "Or should I say, as residents of Zion?" There were a few weak chuckles.

I looked out beyond the tiny headquarters building. The area looked pretty bleak and barren, not a tree in sight. But then, as a "resident of Zion," I was already used to that. We were all then divided into teams to push handcarts filled with our sleeping bags and backpacks, some food, and a little water that would be available in addition to the water trailer. Of course, I chose to walk with Jen. There were also two boys from another ward, and two girls from yet another. I was glancing at my watch, which I wasn't supposed to be wearing, when Sister Clawson, the missionary lady, came up to me with a baby doll. She thrust it at me.

"What's this?" I said.

"Several of the older girls are being chosen to be mothers," Sister Clawson replied. "Many of the women who crossed the plains had to carry babies in addition to pushing the handcarts."

My mouth fell open. I took the doll and tried to hold it while testing whether or not I'd still be able to push. This was going to be a pain in the butt.

Sister Clawson smiled and moved along to find her next "mother."

"Oh, maybe this'll be fun, after all," said Jen, eyeing my baby jealously.

"If I'm married," I replied, "do I get to have sex around the campfire with my husband tonight?"

Jen giggled. "You're so bad." One of the boys assigned to our cart winked at me. I'd seen him a time or two at stake events and thought he was cute, but I wasn't sure he was all that active, because there were lots of activities he should have been at but wasn't. Maybe the Trek was his way of becoming more faithful.

Soon we were off, singing "for some must push and some must pull" as we went. It was already hot. As it turned out, while I tried to hold my baby with one arm and push with the other, this was just too awkward, and most of the time, I just walked. One of the girls from the other ward who were with our handcart said loudly to the other, "Why does *she* get the baby?"

The other girl replied, just as loudly, "Because she looks so matronly." Then both girls sniggered.

That was offset slightly during one of our breaks, when the boy who'd winked at me earlier came in back and said, "I'd let you carry *my* baby anytime." He'd been looking over his shoulder at me and making cute comments the whole trip. After his latest remark, he casually scratched at his crotch and grinned.

"Well, I never!" said the girl who'd called me matronly.

"At this rate, you never will," said the boy. Then he offered his hand to me. "Roger," he said.

"Melanie."

He leaned over and whispered. "Tonight after everyone's asleep, I'll come over to your sleeping bag."

"How will you find me in the dark?"

"They'll keep a few lights on so we can find our way to the bathrooms."

I nodded. "And what will you do once you find me?"

"We'll just kiss tonight," he whispered. "It's only our first date." He paused and glanced over at the girl looking haughtily at us. "But on the *third* night..." His voice trailed away, and I smiled. Of course I would never do anything more than kiss on a date in any event, but it was fun to feel so bold and decadent. Even the chaperones had to sleep at some point. This trek might be more fun than I'd thought.

We continued on our walk, very slowly, between one and two miles an hour. That was almost worse than walking at a normal pace, but with the handcarts, it was difficult to go very quickly. I noticed one girl from the handcart in front of us had to make frequent trips to the porta-john wagon. I wondered if she was menstruating. How awful and embarrassing. Thank god it wasn't my time of the month, I thought. How miserable *that* must have been in the old days. And as disgusting as the porta-johns themselves were, I was grateful we weren't being expected to use the alternative the pioneers had.

We stopped again for lunch, and while I wasn't exhausted, I realized I'd be pretty tired by the end of the day. Doing this walking all day every day for three solid months truly must have been quite the ordeal, I thought.

"Hey, my clothes are all dirty," said a boy from one of the other handcarts. "I fell down back there."

"Well, you'll just have to stay dirty for the next three days," said one of the adults near him. "There were certainly no washers and dryers back in the day."

The rest of the afternoon plodded along uneventfully. Earlier in the morning, we'd sung lots of pioneer songs and hymns. Now everyone was too tired. Even just standing in this heat for all those hours would have been exhausting, much less walking while pushing or pulling a handcart. Or carrying a baby. I began to realize I was one of the lucky ones. A doll wasn't as heavy as that handcart.

"Wanna trade?" asked Jen, eyeing my baby enviously. "Mothers back in pioneer days probably traded."

Jen looked really tired, so I agreed. She took the baby with a smile, and I assumed her place pushing the cart. Sure enough, it wasn't as fun as the bishop had made it sound during his encouraging talk at church a couple of weeks ago. I took the baby back around 5:00, and though there was still plenty of light left, the commander of the group, a man from another ward, soon called a halt for the day. There was a soft cheer.

Before long, a couple of minivans showed up, and the leaders organized the kids to start cooking. It turned out that two of the handcarts were carrying barbecues. "We don't want to start a wildfire," one of the men explained. The boys ended up doing most of the cooking, hamburgers and roasted potatoes. It was a little strange having the potatoes in place of French fries, but satisfying enough. I thought it odd that indoors, women were always expected to be in the kitchen, but being outdoors suddenly made cooking masculine, and the boys fought over the grill.

"No pickle relish?" asked a boy, looking forlornly at his dry hamburger. "Those pioneers really did rough it."

I had to hold the baby in my lap while I ate, and Jen kept giggling every time I'd let the doll slide down. Once I found myself resting my elbows on it. Even Roger laughed then. "I see why so many infants died along the trail," he said. I stuck out my tongue at him.

"I want to see more of that tongue later," he said.

The girl who'd called me matronly glared at us. I simply said, "There won't be *that* many lights. You'll have to feel your way around."

17

"I'm up for feeling my way." He made a motion as if squeezing a melon in the air. I instinctively put my arm across my chest.

After supper was over and everything had been cleaned up, it was still light, though getting late. Everyone gathered around the elderly missionary couple who'd apparently brought lawn chairs along on one of the handcarts. The rest of us were sitting on the ground. "Time for some pioneer stories," announced Brother Clawson.

"I know some of you have sore feet," he said, "but did you know there were many people, especially children and teenagers whose feet kept growing too fast for their parents to keep buying them new shoes, who actually walked the entire way barefoot?"

There was a low gasp from the crowd. "Many of them arrived in the Salt Lake Valley with their feet all bloodied. That's how much they cared about getting to the Promised Land."

I looked about at the dreary landscape.

"And there were lots of young people your age who were real heroes on some of these treks," Brother Clawson went on. "You've probably heard of the Martin handcart company, who were so anxious to get to Salt Lake that they started out too late in the season rather than wait a whole year. Of course, the snows came early, and they suffered terribly and were finally stranded. When Brigham Young heard about their plight, he sent a rescue party, which reached the group at Sweetwater River in Wyoming.

"The group had to cross that big, icy river, and most of them simply weren't up to it. So three teenage boys, boys your age, carried almost every single member of the Martin party across that river by hand. They saved dozens of lives." He paused dramatically. "But all three boys died later of complications they suffered for their heroism." There was silence among the group. "That's what being a hero means, doing the right thing regardless of the consequences." He looked out at all of us. "Do *you* always do the right thing?"

The stories continued for another forty minutes, until it really did start to get dark. I had been expecting a campfire at some point. Camping always seemed to revolve around campfires, so I was surprised when the leaders brought out several battery-charged lanterns and set them up at strategic intervals. The boys were directed to lay out their sleeping bags on one side of the line of handcarts, and the girls were directed to the opposite side.

"Time for snakes to slide in with us to keep warm," muttered Jen.

I rarely went to bed this early, but I had to admit, I was quite tired, and I still had two more days of this to go through. Jen and I chatted in our bags for a few minutes, but then I could tell she had fallen asleep, and I wasn't far behind her. While I'd been out of gymnastics for over a year now, I dreamed about doing hours of gymnastics drills.

Sometime later, I felt someone nudging me. "Huh?" I said.

"Shh! It's me, Roger."

I awoke almost immediately, astonished he'd actually come over. To my surprise, he didn't sit or lie down beside me but lay directly on top of my sleeping bag. "What do you think you're doing?" I hissed.

"It's perfectly safe," Roger whispered back. "We have this barrier between us. It'll be okay." And with that, he put his lips against mine and kissed me. Although I'd been dating boys for a year, I'd never kissed. Most boys only took me on one date, so there was never any time to work up to greater intimacy. I knew my Mom didn't want me kissing at all, saying I should wait to kiss for my first time over the altar in the temple, but I'd been wondering about it for ages and couldn't resist when the opportunity was thrust upon me.

"Shh," said Roger a few minutes later. "You're moaning."

There was a fumbling attempt at groping through the sleeping bag, but the material was too thick to allow much satisfaction. Still, the kissing alone was enough. Roger lay on top of me for a full thirty minutes. Finally, he pulled back and whispered, "That was Date Number One. Just wait till tomorrow night."

I was glad Mom had insisted I come on this trip.

Roger crept off again to his side of the handcarts, and while I tried to think about kissing, I was soon back asleep.

In the morning, I was dying to tell Jen what had happened, but there just wasn't enough privacy. After a quick breakfast of bacon and eggs, we all gathered our belongings back onto the handcarts and took off again. It felt a little odd not having a real goal. The pioneers could feel every day they were just that much closer to Salt Lake, but we were merely wandering about the Deseret Land and Livestock farm simply to be wandering. I felt more like a Jew following Moses in the desert for forty years than a Mormon pioneer.

We sang pioneer songs and hymns again, Jen and I trading off carrying the baby. It got to be where I started to hate the damn thing. Even pushing the cart felt more useful than carrying a piece of plastic. At least this wasn't one of those new fancy dolls that "messed" its diaper. I was sure the leaders had considered it, just to make the trek more miserable, but whatever their reasons were for deciding against it, I was grateful.

"Hey," said Roger during a break. "Why don't you come pull the cart with me for a bit while Tim here goes in back and helps push?"

We tried that, and Roger and I were able to talk for about ten minutes, but it soon became apparent I was a pusher, not a puller, and Tim and I switched places again. "Using a spiritual Church outing to flirt with a boy," muttered the girl who'd called me matronly. I still hadn't asked her name. "No wonder you ended up with a baby."

Jen and I talked about Sunday school for a while, how we almost fell asleep last week until Brother Sidney slapped the table with his Book of Mormon. We talked about Sister Patterson, who was clearly after Brother Sidney, for some unfathomable reason. And then Jen said, "Can I have David now that you have Roger?"

"He's still a non-member," I pointed out.

"I can fix that. He comes to church, doesn't he?"

"Sometimes."

Soon we stopped for lunch, and then we were back walking again. In some ways, today was easier than the day before because I was "in the groove." But in other ways, the walking was becoming very tedious. I was athletic by nature and never minded a good hour-long walk once in a while. But this was hour after hour after hour after hour. My feet tingled the entire time we were on breaks. And there was nothing to look at but short prairie grass as far as the eye could see. That and the back of the handcart in front of me. I was so bored. You could only chat with your best friend just so long before you ran out of things to say. Yesterday, there'd been a buzz about the group even when we weren't singing. Today, there were huge spans of silence, only the sounds of the creaking handcart wheels to fill the air.

We were so tired by dinner that even hot dogs and potato chips couldn't cheer us up very much. The minivans had brought ketchup this time, so supper was quite a treat. I was just too tired to appreciate it. "What you need is a *real* hot dog," said Roger.

"Oh, brother," said the matronly girl in disgust.

We had another session of pioneer stories after supper. Sister Clawson spoke about pioneer girls this time. "Mary Iverson's mother was sick and was tired of drinking melted snow. She asked Mary, who was sixteen, to go find a stream and bring back fresh water. While they were stopped, Mary went to look for a stream, but she was so afraid of the Indians in the area who'd been following them that she got distracted and ended up lost. The snow was up almost to her knees, and by the time she was found, she had frostbite. She never did find the stream to bring back fresh water for her mother, but by the time she got back to the camp, her mother had died anyway. Three of

Mary's brothers and sisters had died in the previous weeks, but now she was left in charge of her one remaining baby brother. They were living on just one ounce of flour a day. When she arrived in Salt Lake, she had her toes amputated. She found a good man who married her and helped raise her brother and their own seven children. She lived a good, gospel-centered life because she crossed those plains and came to Salt Lake."

And I had slipped out to Starbucks two months ago to try my first latte, I thought. I should be ashamed of myself, when my ancestors had been through so much to provide me with the gospel.

The lanterns were up and everyone was in their sleeping bags even earlier than the night before. Jen was saying something to me about wanting to wash her hair when I fell into a deep sleep almost instantly. Sometime in the night, I was only vaguely aware of someone touching me. I opened my eyes, but unlike the previous evening, tonight I was still groggy. Roger was unzipping my sleeping bag and lying down on top of me. His weight felt quite comfortable. I wanted nothing more than to sleep with him lying there. He tried kissing my lips, but I was rather unresponsive, I suppose, so he just kissed my cheeks and then my shoulders.

I did fall asleep again but then suddenly awakened when I felt something entering me. I gasped and was about to cry out when Roger put his lips over mine. We weren't supposed to be doing this, I wanted to say. It hurt a little, and somehow also felt good. His weight and his kisses were sublime. And I felt like a real woman for the first time. I had just decided to push him off anyway, when he groaned and rolled over. He'd only been on top of me a couple of minutes.

"I told you the second date would be better," he whispered.

I wondered what our third date would be like the following evening. After Roger sneaked quietly back to his side of the handcarts, I looked up at the stars and wondered what to do. There was Taurus, I noticed, and Leo. But the stars couldn't distract me for long. I'd just had sex, when two days ago I'd never even kissed a boy. What was I going to do? Should I tell my bishop when I got home? Should I tell my parents? Should I tell Jen?

Or should I just keep my mouth shut? Just because I'd done it once didn't mean I had to do it again. I could still go to the temple. Maybe with Roger when he got back from his mission. I could wait for him.

I was up another twenty minutes reflecting, but then the fatigue of the day settled back in and I fell asleep again.

In the morning after another round of bacon and eggs, I headed for the porta-john trailer. There were two adult men talking. They glanced at me, but since I was still exhausted, I must have looked oblivious. I didn't even realize what they were saying for the first few moments. Then I began to hear.

"I liked the old days better," said one of the men, "when we only had johnnie cake and molasses on these trips, and the trips lasted a whole week, not just three short days. And we pushed the kids to walk farther every day, and we really were able to break their spirits, just like a horse's. You could create a spiritual conversion back then once you broke someone's spirit. Now these kids'll go home thinking they're so great, and go back to being the same rotten kids they were before."

"I'm not rotten," I wanted to say, but then I remembered last night. Maybe I *was* rotten. At the same time, what had happened *almost* seemed like a spiritual experience. Maybe

Roger and I would take our time tonight and I'd learn what it felt like to truly experience love.

The pioneer songs and hymns lasted a little longer this morning, everyone psyched up despite their fatigue, knowing this was the last day. Jen and I ended up tying the baby to my back so I could help push continually along with her. We took two breaks before lunch, and then a long lunch break. "You seem to have a certain glow about you today," said Roger, smiling at me and winking.

I stuck out my tongue.

"I want to see more of that later."

The girl who'd called me matronly snorted.

I was just dying to talk openly with Jen, but I realized I might not be able to tell her even after we got home. She might say something to someone. As we trudged across the hills after lunch, I kept sneaking a look at my watch. Soon this would all be over. Soon I'd be home.

But even sooner would be tonight's date.

"I can't wait to take a bath," said Jen.

"Think our folks will expect us to go to church Sunday?" I asked.

"Oh, they'll expect it, but they're not going to get it." She laughed. "It's the least I can get out of this."

About three in the afternoon, during one of our breaks, Brother Clawson came over to me while I was sipping some water and flicking some in Roger's face. "Your baby has just died," he said calmly.

"What?"

"It happened often during these treks. Your baby died, and now you have to bury it." He handed me a spade. I took it and looked at him in confusion. "We used to make the girls dig the graves with sticks," he explained, "but we use spades now. Go dig a grave, and you can have this young man…" He pointed at Roger. "…say a blessing over it."

Brother Clawson kept walking through the crowd, picking out several other "mothers" who'd just lost their babies. I couldn't believe what had just happened.

"I'm so sorry for your loss," said Jen. I couldn't tell if she was serious or joking.

"Come on," said Roger. "I'll help you dig."

We walked off about thirty yards from the main group and knelt in the prairie grass. Roger took the spade and started digging. "Gives us a chance to be alone," he said. He looked at me and smiled broadly. "I really like you, Melanie."

I smiled back. "I'm glad we were on the same team." I wanted to ask if he'd call me, but I didn't want to sound desperate.

It took us half an hour, but we finally buried the doll, and Roger even managed to offer a brief prayer, despite the fact that none of this was real. I admired him for it. Maybe we had sinned once, but we'd be good from now on and get married in the temple after he came back from overseas.

We joined the others, who'd simply been grateful to have a longer than normal break, and we set off on our last segment of the journey. We met up with the minivans around 5:15 and had our last supper, pork and beans with potato salad and tiny sausages.

I wished I had a Coke.

There were no pioneer stories this evening. Tonight was saved up for a testimony meeting. For a while, it seemed like almost everyone in the entire party planned to bear their testimony. I thought the meeting would never end. There were tearful speeches about "finally understanding the sacrifices our forefathers made" and "feeling closer to Heavenly Father and Jesus Christ than ever before." The adults looked on, almost smirking rather than smiling.

But eventually, around 9:00, Brother Clawson offered a prayer, and we headed for our sleeping bags. As excited as I was to see Roger again, I was still completely exhausted and decided to take a nap before his visit. Like before, I awakened later to find him kneeling over me. I pulled him down and kissed him. He unzipped my bag, spread my legs, and entered me again. I wrapped my arms around his back and luxuriated thoroughly in the experience. When he'd finished several minutes later, I whispered, "Do it again."

Roger laughed softly. "I can only come twice, you know."

"Well, how many times have you come?" I laughed.

"I already did it with Sue once."

I stared at him in the darkness, hardly able to make out his face. "Who's Sue?"

"That girl who doesn't like you."

"You had sex with *her* this evening?" I said, astounded at what I was hearing.

"Yes, but I picked you to be last because I knew it would take longer. I like you better."

I unwrapped my arms from around Roger's back.

"Can I call you next Saturday?" he whispered.

"After going out with Sue on Friday?" I whispered back.

He laughed. "What do you care what I do Friday, as long as I'm with you on Saturday?" He caressed my face. "We're here to learn to live like the pioneers. The pioneers practiced polygamy, you know."

"I think you better go back to your side of the camp."

"Wait a second," said Roger, and he did wait a few moments before speaking again, fondling himself. "I think I can come a third time." He put his hands between my legs.

I sighed and opened up, letting Roger inside again. It took him fifteen minutes this time. I lay back and stared up at the stars, trying to find Scorpio as Roger pumped away, and looking forward to the long trip back to Salt Lake in the morning.

# Gardening without Deet

I rotated the faucet handle to the left and felt the hose stiffen in my hands. Then I walked to the furthermost point in the front yard and twisted the tarnished nozzle. A strong spray hit the huge rhododendron bush, bloomless at this time of year but still magnificent. I turned the nozzle toward the roots.

Brother and Sister Maberly had hired me in March to mow their yard and take care of the weeding around their plants. As I was a fairly normal sixteen-year-old, it was all the work I wanted to do. Soon I had three agreements with different ward members of the Seattle Second Ward. I began spending a couple of hours at each property on Saturdays, and with travel to and from, it was pretty much a full day.

Only we'd had a hotter than average summer, with highs in the mid to upper 80's most days, hitting 90 or above all too frequently. Most summers, we only hit 90 a mere three times. This summer, we'd reached it a full eleven times, and it was still just the first week of August. People thought of Seattle as rainy, but they didn't realize we went months with hardly a drop during the summer. This season was turning out to be drier than usual. Now two of the families I mowed for also had me come over three days a week after school to water.

And yes, I did go to school in the summer. It turns out I wasn't the brightest bulb in the socket.

Not even bright enough to come up with a good metaphor.

But I didn't really mind school, even if I didn't excel there. Something about learning at least a little every day was kind of satisfying.

I moved over to the daisies, and then to the rosemary, then to the Japanese pine, and on to the purple-colored wild rose bush. The Maberlys also tried to heed the Church's suggestion to grow their own vegetables, so I watered the two tomato bushes, the three yellow crooked neck squash, the four carrots, and the five red onions. I saw a blemish on one of the tomato plants and smiled.

I suppose it was sinful of me, but I wanted Heavenly Father to send a plague upon the whole world. We were in the middle of the world's sixth mass extinction. Most of the other events had been caused by comet impacts or supervolcanoes, but this one was entirely man-made. I wanted God to kill off a billion of us in the next year. Even that would only gain us an extra decade, but I was afraid the Millennium might be too far away for life as we knew it to continue, if God didn't intervene now.

He'd done it during the Middle Ages, hadn't he, sending the bubonic plague to wipe out a third of Europe and Asia? Civilization had survived just fine, perhaps even benefitted because of it. We needed God to do the same thing now, before it was too late.

I sprayed the grass in the back yard, and the hydrangea, and the day lilies. Then I turned the faucet to the right and headed for my Dad's truck. He didn't let me drive on dates, or even to the store, but he did let me use his truck for work.

"Was that a half hour, Kip?" asked Sister Maberly, coming to the front door to peer out as I walked down the front walk.

"Thirty-one minutes," I replied. "I always like to do a little extra." I tipped an imaginary hat.

Sister Maberly laughed and closed the door, and I hopped in the truck and headed to my next stop, the home of the Clarks. They had mostly grass in front and only a boring line of nondescript bushes right against the house. They'd have been better off buying a sprinkler, but they had hired me, and who was I to turn down good money? I still had my mission to prepare for, if I lived that long.

"Please, Heavenly Father," I prayed as I pulled up to the Clarks' house, "if I'm bad for asking you to kill a billion people, feel free to take me, too."

I didn't knock but got right to work, turning on the hose and starting my watering. The Clarks had a glade in their spacious back yard, and the place was always full of mosquitoes. By the time I finished the front and reached the back, it was getting to be that time of day when the mosquitoes were happiest. I couldn't say it was actually dusk. It was only 7:00, another two hours before sundown, but I could hear the high-pitched whining around my ears. On Mondays, I watered earlier, of course, to be back at the house in time for Family Home Evening, but on the other two weekdays, I tried to wait till the worst of the heat was over, so all the water wouldn't evaporate but have a chance to soak in after I left. That meant mosquito time at the Clarks' today. I felt the hairs on my arm being touched by one of the noisy insects and sighed.

If only some new deadly disease could be carried by mosquitoes, I thought. Something no one would be able to escape easily.

If only pneumonic plague could get established, something spread by air.

"Hi, Kip," said Brother Clark, coming out to check on me. "How are you doing today?"

"I'm fine, Brother Clark. You?"

"Oh, we're all good. Not even a cold in the family. You know with six kids I can't say that very often." He chuckled.

I wondered why with six children he had to hire help for his yard. Probably because they were upper middle class. They didn't do peasant work.

"How's Janet?" I asked. That was his fifteen-year-old daughter.

Brother Clark laughed again. "Spray some of that cold water on yourself," he said. "She won't be old enough to date for another year."

I directed the hose at my head, giving myself a refreshingly cool drenching, and Brother Clark laughed again. "Crazy kid." He turned around and went back in the house.

I spent a few extra minutes in the back yard spraying, knowing it would leave little puddles for the mosquitoes to lay eggs in. I saw one of the insects on my wrist and watched as it sucked blood for almost thirty seconds before flying away.

I climbed back in the truck and turned on the radio. A report about the tensions between Russia and the West. Over a thousand people killed in Gaza. 100% of the state of California in severe drought. Aquifers in Colorado and Utah drying up. July of this year the warmest worldwide on record. Fifteen people dead of heatstroke in Japan from soaring temperatures. Congress on vacation after the least effective session ever. Ebola out of control in Africa.

That last story piqued my interest, but only about 700 people had died so far. You couldn't save the world by killing a measly 700 people. Some of the infected would have to travel by plane to other countries and spread the disease. It was a nasty way to go, but it was relatively quick. It was important that whatever plague Heavenly Father sent act fast enough not to cause unnecessary suffering, and also fast enough not to use up too much money in treating it. AIDS, for instance, took years to kill and cost far too much money per patient. That wasn't going to work.

But Ebola? Maybe. Though it was a little more gruesome than I'd have liked. Still, civilization could handle losing a billion people. Maybe even two billion. We'd only be going back to the world population of the 1970's, when things were already bad enough. Perhaps God should kill three or four billion.

That might be too disruptive, unless it happened over a twenty-year period, to give us time to adjust. Heavenly Father was smart enough to handle the details.

I scratched at the mosquito bite on my wrist.

I parked the truck in the garage, two inches from the rear wall, just the way Dad liked it, and headed into the house.

"You're filthy," said Mom, pointing at me. "Take your shoes off, and go upstairs immediately and take a shower, and throw those dirty clothes in the hamper. I swear, I spend more money cleaning up after you than you bring home from those little jobs of yours."

I felt a pang of guilt at the words, thinking of fracking companies irreversibly polluting billions of gallons of water. I didn't want to add to the problem.

"Please, Heavenly Father," I said as the shower head sprayed down upon me, "I know you can resurrect the dead. You can bring back all the species we kill off. But I don't *want* you to do that. I want you to keep us from killing everything off in the first place." I soaped up my body quickly, and as the shower was my only opportunity to beat off, I did that quickly, too, and then turned the water to cold and luxuriated in the feel of it falling powerfully on my head and chest.

"I know we have free will," I continued, "and I know you have to let us do what we'll do. But you intervened in the Middle Ages. That means you can do it again. And you killed twenty million with the flu in 1918. You can do this." I turned off the water and pulled back the shower curtain. "You can do this," I repeated.

"Who are you talking to?" shouted my brother Carl through the closed bathroom door.

"Practicing my talk for Sunday," I shouted back. I dried off and pulled on my boxer briefs. I looked at myself in the mirror. Five foot eleven, with firm muscles, a flat stomach, and a nice bulge in my briefs.

I wished I were dead. If my death could help save the world, why wouldn't I be willing? Most Christians got it wrong when they talked about how Jesus was so great because he died for our sins. Dying for someone wasn't hard. What Jesus had done was *suffer* for our sins, atone for them. That had happened in the Garden of Gethsemane, not on the cross. That's where the truly difficult act had occurred.

I didn't know that I was willing to suffer. I wanted a quick death. But I was certainly willing to die, do the easy part.

If I didn't die, what terrible miseries awaited me in just ten or fifteen years? Whatever was going to happen was going to happen in my lifetime, not in some vague, distant future. Why couldn't people see? Why didn't people do anything?

I remembered hearing a talk at church about a pilot of a small plane flying over mountain roads. He watched as a car drove recklessly, going too far into the other lane around corners. The driver of the car couldn't see the heavy truck coming the other way, just a few feet away around the bend. But the pilot saw the disaster before it even happened. The speaker said that was the difference between how we mortals saw life and how Heavenly Father saw life. God had a better perspective.

But *I* could see what was about to happen, and I was no god. Just a dumb kid.

"Heavenly Father, I know the deaths will probably be random," I said softly so Carl wouldn't hear, "but if you could tailor your plague to kill the jerks, that would be really great. But however you do it, we need you, Heavenly Father. We need you."

I pulled on my blue jeans and T-shirt, and I combed my hair. Then I headed back down the stairs to the kitchen, where Mom was waiting with my late supper. Mormons were supposed to eat together as families, but these three weeknights

I worked, Mom made sure to sit with me while I ate, so I still felt a part of the family.

"So, what did you learn in school today?" Mom asked, setting a dish of Irish stew in front of me.

I thought of the potato famine that had killed two million.

I started to bow my head, but my mother interrupted. "It's already been blessed," she said.

I added a little pepper even before tasting it, took a bite, and with my mouth half full, started to answer her earlier question. Mom wagged her finger and I swallowed before continuing. "We talked about wind power. And generating energy from waves."

Mom shrugged. "Sounds a little boring. They should make learning more fun." She looked at her watch.

I smiled sadly and took another bite of stew. "You can kill my Mom, too, if you have to," I prayed silently. "But please spare Janet. And please help her to have kids that will grow up in a wonderful new world."

I thought about the dreary prospect of teaching the uninterested masses about the hard work we had to do immediately. Was that like atoning? It was easier to pray for a plague.

Mom looked like she was straining to hear the sounds of the television show drifting in from the living room. She forced a smile and asked me another question about school. I told her about the new theorem I learned in Geometry today, and then she decided I could eat the rest of my meal alone.

# Vitamin-Rich Baptisms for the Dead

"How would you like to baptize your fellow missionaries?" asked President Ashworth, my mission president here in Dallas. "Might be the only time you get to baptize anyone else before you go home." He chuckled. I had baptized three people before being called as Assistant to the President and moving to the mission home last year.

"I think it would be great," I replied, "but I thought temple workers did all the baptisms."

"We'll ask them to let you baptize. It'll be a great honor. Something I think a dedicated AP deserves to have one month before he goes home."

"Well, I certainly appreciate it, President."

He clapped me on the back. "Anything for the one elder I can count on not to masturbate."

I could feel my face turning red, though really, by this point, you'd think I'd be used to it. Just over a year ago, when I was not quite halfway through my mission, the president had given a serious talk during one of our zone conferences. After excusing the sisters from the session, he'd said, "Elders, I want to talk to you about the sin of masturbation. It's a serious problem here in the mission. Now some of you have been wise and intelligent and come to me about it. That's what the Lord wants. This isn't something you can overcome by yourselves. Others of you have had the audacity to believe you can take care of it by yourself. But you need me to help you take care of it. In our interviews today, I want every elder who has a problem with masturbation to talk to me about it frankly. I want to hear everything. It's your only chance to become pure again, be forgiven for this heinous sin, and get the Holy Ghost back in your lives so you can baptize as you've been called to do."

I was just a senior companion then, and as the interviews progressed, it turned out that I was the last in line to go in the bishop's office. I told President Ashworth about a family my companion and I were teaching, about a recent Companion Inventory when my junior companion told me he didn't believe in the Book of Mormon, and how I'd borne my testimony so strongly to him that he was crying by the time I'd finished. I didn't tell the president that I didn't really have a testimony myself yet, that I was simply following the commandment to testify my belief *until* I firmly believed.

As I did every day to the non-members we met, trying to convince them I had something truly special to share.

Maybe I did have something special, I hoped, and maybe someday I'd understand that more fully. That's why I was out here serving a mission. My father had told me, "You're not there just to convert others. If the only convert you bring to the Church is you, you'll have had a successful mission. This is about *your* spiritual health."

So I told the president about how I'd gotten four referrals the week before.

Finally, when it seemed like the interview was almost over, President Ashworth looked at his watch and said, "There's nothing else you need to talk to me about?" He gave me a piercing stare.

"I don't think so," I replied carefully.

"Nothing about what I said during the conference?" he prodded.

Now I did masturbate occasionally, of course. The problem with confessing is that I liked to do it with my left thumb stuck up my ass. I could hardly tell the president that. But he kept pushing and pushing, not taking "no comment" for an answer. After a full ten minutes of badgering, I finally broke down and told him all the details. I expected him to be disgusted, but to my surprise, he smiled broadly.

"Elder Keller," he said, "don't think you've shocked me. The Lord already revealed your problem to me. He just needed you to humble yourself in front of me before he would allow me to call you as Assistant to the President."

"Assistant to the President?" I said weakly, my face still red. "But I've never even been District Leader or Zone Leader yet."

"The Lord calls whom he will call," said the president solemnly. "There's just one last test."

My heart started beating faster.

"Let's go back out to the group." He stood up and I followed him to the door. We were meeting in one of the local church buildings. The other elders were hanging out in the Cultural Hall, all in their suits, though some looked as if they wished they were playing basketball. The sisters were in the chapel. Normally, we all mixed, but the president had segregated us because of the delicate nature of his talk on masturbation. He had one last talk to give to the sisters, he told us, after he sent us elders on our way.

I didn't think I wanted to hear that talk, either. I'd overheard some of the sisters say that during private interviews, the president asked them some very inappropriate things. Things I didn't want to think about.

Of course, those were just rumors.

We entered the Cultural Hall, and everyone stopped talking as President Ashworth cleared his throat. His hand was on my shoulder. "Elders," he said, "I've just called Elder Keller to be the new junior AP." There was a moment of impressed and jealous silence. "But he'll need your help staying worthy of the calling." I started sweating and held my breath. "Elder Keller has a problem with masturbation, like many of you." All eyes were now on me, and I wished I could disappear into the wooden-tiled floor. "He does it in the shower." Oh, my god, he wasn't going to mention the thumb, was he? "So I want every one of you, every time you run into him, to ask him if he's still worthy. I believe that with all of you checking up on him regularly, he'll stay true to his temple vows."

I wanted to die, drop dead right there and then. My face was so hot I thought it would burst into flame right in the Cultural Hall. The president turned to me, and I forced a smile. "Thank you, President Ashworth," I managed.

He smiled again, too, even more broadly than before. "You've passed the final test," he said. "You'll make a great AP. Your humility will be your greatest asset."

I wasn't sure that humility and humiliation were the same thing, but I continued smiling.

Sure enough, the elders regularly quizzed me, more as a joke than out of any desire to see me lead a righteous life, but I had to admit, knowing I was going to be asked did help me stop masturbating. A full year had passed since I'd abused myself. I hadn't baptized any more people, of course, so I wasn't sure the Holy Ghost was residing in me any more regularly. I sometimes felt rather dead serving all these months without baptizing, but if I were to be honest, I'd felt a little dead even during those early months when I *was* baptizing. I wondered if it was a sin to feel this way during the two years that were supposed to be the highlight of my youth. I exercised every day, ate my broccoli and carrots, and tried to live a good, upstanding life. I still felt like an apostate most of the time, starting to doubt the Book of Mormon myself a little more each time I read it, but with masturbation crossed off the list, I knew that, despite my weaknesses, I had to be heading in the right direction. And it did certainly feel good not to have to lie or hide, and to be able to partake of the sacrament without hesitation.

Assuming there really was such a thing as the Atonement.

Stop it, Elder, and do some push-ups, I commanded myself. That was my answer to all my daily doubts, and I had by now developed some very nice upper body strength.

The real problem came when I had to accompany the president throughout the mission to different zone conferences. Every single time, he'd have me stand and tell the story of how I stopped masturbating, and there'd be a moment of silence as everyone stared at me. Somehow, being the poster boy for clean living didn't feel like a victory. I began to wonder if the missionary rule to work 60 hours a week, and my own personal directive to help out with these never-ending conferences, was to keep us too busy to realize…what? That we were missing out on sinning? Missing out on life? I really wasn't sure. Even after I became senior AP, my abstinence proclamations continued.

Sometimes, I thought about sinning again, just to have the pressure off. But the president had said to me in private once, "Guilt is a form of preventive medicine," and like it or not, it seemed to work.

Now here I was with only one month to go before returning home to La Jolla. I'd start back to college right away, marry within six months, and never have to worry about masturbating again. And this special treat of doing baptisms for the dead in the temple was just the thing to give me the boost I'd need to stay pure after returning to civilian life.

The mission minivan and the ZL and DL cars were all packed with young men as we started our convoy to the temple. Only the elders were attending today, our regular P-Day. The sisters were told to spend their Preparation Day cooking cupcakes to serve us after we returned.

Once in the temple, I followed the president and the other elders to the men's dressing room. I put on a special pair of garments, needing my own to be dry when I finished the baptisms. Then I put on a white jumpsuit. All the elders were laughing and joking about adding these baptisms to their mission total. "The youth groups usually only get to have fifteen baptisms per person," said the president, "but the temple workers are going to allow us to do twenty per elder." He turned to me and clapped me on the back. "With over ninety elders here today, you'll be baptizing eighteen hundred people!" He tousled my hair and asked, "Are you up to it?"

I nodded, but realizing just how long that would take, even at ten seconds per baptism, I thought maybe I'd better hurry to the bathroom before we started. I ran in, unzipped my jumpsuit, and let go with a stream. Just as I was finishing, the president came up beside me and said, "Let's hurry things along. We don't want to be here all day." I put my penis back in my garments and zipped back up.

And that's when it happened. A last few dribbles of urine gushed out because I hadn't been able to finish in peace. To my horror, I saw them seep through the thin garment and almost-as-thin jumpsuit. It wasn't just a wet spot, though; it was a bright *yellow* wet spot. I took my vitamins daily.

"President, I can't go out there like this," I spluttered. "Let me change real quick."

"Elder Keller, you've delayed us enough as it is. And I want to get back for Sister Ternley's cupcakes. Let's get to the font."

"But President…"

"You need to control that thing at *all* times, not just when you're feeling randy. Let's go."

I was mortified, but then, I realized I'd made a habit out of being mortified for the past year, and I suddenly wondered why I thought that was a good thing, why *anyone* thought that was a good thing. I remembered the talks and pamphlets by Boyd K. Packer, and how I'd spent most of my youth feeling shamed. I knew my companion, the junior AP, still masturbated, as did most of the rest of the mission office staff. My companion said he beat off once a day for health reasons. I knew most of the other missionaries throughout the mission still masturbated as well. If only one person out of a hundred was truly abstinent, and those other ninety-nine were still temple-recommend holders, still holders of the Melchizedek Priesthood, still missionaries serving volunteer missions, still baptizers, weren't those other ninety-nine still decent people? And if even the most decent people on Earth were still masturbating, wasn't trying to stamp it out kind of like trying to stop the rain from falling?

It was going to happen, no matter how embarrassed the practitioners were.

And if that were the case, why devote so much energy to a lost cause?

Then it hit me. The point wasn't to get young men to stop masturbating. The point was to get them to feel so depraved that they would do absolutely anything else asked of them to prove their worthiness.

Like standing up five hours straight baptizing missionaries in the names of dead people, when I could be in my room relaxing on my one day off, listening to music the only time during the week it was allowed, even if it was nothing more than the Mormon Tabernacle Choir. It all just felt like busy work, keeping us so occupied doing "righteous" things during our free time that we didn't realize...what? That we were wasting two years of our lives?

That we were wasting our *entire* lives?

I suddenly felt very angry, a year's worth of sexual repression fighting to get out. I thought about carrying a Bible or Book of Mormon with me to the font, to cover my embarrassment, but I was so irritated now that I didn't want to cover myself at all. I walked out, ahead of President Ashworth, and headed straight to the baptismal font. As I stood to step in, I saw a couple of the elders point and heard them giggle.

"Don't worry," I said, "it's not pee." I paused just a second and then added, "It's cum. I get so excited being with other men in the temple." I looked about for a moment and then announced, "President Ashworth here asks all the sister missionaries not to get married after their missions, that they should save themselves to be his wives in the Celestial Kingdom." There was a gasp and suddenly all the talking and laughing stopped. "So I'd like to ask all of you not to get married after your missions, either, and save yourselves for me, until gay marriage is finally accepted by the Church."

I stepped in the font and raised my right arm to the square. "Who's first?" I asked. What I'd said about me wasn't true, of course—I was straight as an arrow—but I simply felt the need to say something outrageous, "for health reasons." What I'd said about President Ashworth, on the other hand…

The man looked as if he were about to explode, redder than I'd ever been even during the worst of the masturbation talks I'd had to give. It was worth being sent home a month early to see that face. He pointed at me and jerked his finger toward the dressing room, and I was just about to climb out of the font when one of the new elders spoke up.

"I'll be first," he said timidly. He didn't look especially gay and probably wasn't. He just said yes because…well, I don't know why he said yes. I just figured he had his reasons. He stepped forward and into the font, and we assumed the baptismal position. As President Ashworth looked on in anger, and the other elders in confusion, I baptized my first missionary.

There were over ninety more who followed.

# Equity for Monica

Monica sighed and pulled down a jar of Newman's Own Sweet Onion and Roasted Garlic spaghetti sauce from the cupboard. As good as it was, Raymond always liked her to add some chopped onions and rosemary from their yard, and he insisted she cook the already cooked sauce for at least two hours before dinner. Monica didn't really mind, of course. It wasn't as if heating up spaghetti sauce was difficult, and they had some type of Italian meal five nights of every week—fettucine alfredo, bow tie with parmesan, spaghetti with meatballs, beef ravioli, four cheese tortellini—whatever she could do to create some variety, but always lasagna on Sundays after church.

She struggled with the lid and was just about to pull out a lid-opener from the drawer when she heard the doorbell. Monica put the jar down and walked to the front of the house, peering through the peep hole before reaching for the door handle. It looked like two Chicago police officers.

Oh, dear Lord! There wasn't a shooting at the high school, was there? Monica jerked the door open quickly. "Yes?" she said anxiously.

One of the officers was a black man in his thirties. The other was a white woman who barely looked out of her teens. The man cleared his throat. "Ma'am, do you know a Raymond Aldrich?"

"Yes?" Her heart was beating faster.

The officer shifted his feet. "I'm afraid there's been an accident."

"Is he dead?" Monica blurted out.

"I'm…I'm afraid so. Looks like he was texting and stepped in front of a bus."

Monica almost laughed. Raymond was always such a doofus. Then she remembered how horrible a thing this actually was.

"Oh, no," she murmured.

"There's never an easy way to tell someone something as awful as this," interjected the female officer. "Do you have a church you attend? Perhaps we could contact your pastor to be with you."

The bishop? thought Monica. Even on good days, he was insensitive. She shook her head.

"Your husband's pretty badly mangled, I'm afraid," the male officer continued.

Monica swallowed.

"But they'll still want you to come down and make a positive identification of the body. And of course, you'll need to start making arrangements." The officer motioned toward his car.

"Oh, I can't come now," Monica protested. "My son will be home from school soon. Can I come in a couple of hours? I need some time to process this before I see Raymond."

The man glanced over at the woman and then looked back at Monica. "Sure, I understand." He paused and then added lamely, "I'm sorry."

"Thank you." Monica nodded and closed the door softly. She leaned against it and let out a deep breath. Raymond was dead. After twenty-five years of marriage. She looked about at the huge foyer, the cavernous living room, the elaborate stairs leading upwards. This whole huge house was hers now. Hers and Gatlin's. He was a senior with four months left till graduation, already planning on his mission. How would he take it?

His mission. Monica knew that Raymond had taken out a $500,000 life insurance policy to make sure the kids could all serve missions and get their college degrees. Darren was twenty-four and finished with both, having just scored a teaching fellowship for the Masters program he'd be starting soon. Serena was twenty-one and in the middle of her mission to Ireland. She wouldn't even be allowed to come home for the funeral.

But there was plenty of money to help them all finish whatever they needed to finish. The house was paid off. There was $50,000 in CDs, and another $15,000 in savings. It wasn't enough to support Monica the rest of her life, but it was enough that she didn't have to worry for a while.

The kids all loved their dad, thought Monica. They'd be pretty broken up. He always had a kind, supportive word for them.

Not like for Monica, she thought. Just last week, he'd motioned to her stomach and said disgustedly, "Looks like you're about to have an alien burst out."

Yes, she was fat, but it wasn't as if he were some great athlete himself. She rubbed her stomach now and thought. Maybe she could join a gym next week, meet some people outside their Mormon congregation. Monica was tired of only knowing her family and other Church members. She walked slowly back to the kitchen and saw the jar of tomato sauce sitting on the counter.

Her stomach growled. Shouldn't she have lost her appetite, she wondered? She'd just lost her husband. She could hear Raymond's voice as if he were in the kitchen with her right now. "There were no comps on the AVM, so I had to pull one from a different company. Only two comps there, so we had to ask the borrower to pay for an appraisal. Boy, was he mad."

"Uh-huh."

"The loan officer didn't add T & I, and when I caught it, it changed the debt to income so that it was too high."

"That's too bad."

"The loan officer still can't get me a signed borrower's authorization, and we're already about to go to Underwriting!"

"Oh, dear."

"The originator input the borrower's address incorrectly, and I ended up mailing disclosures to the wrong address!"

"How frustrating."

"The LTV is 101, and they want an exception!"

Dear Lord, how many times had Monica thought about stabbing her eardrums with a pencil before Raymond came home for dinner and started blathering on about equity loans? But really, what did *she* have to offer? She shopped and cleaned and prepared her Sunday school lesson. She was more boring than he was. At least he got to ride the train into town. At least he got to talk to people.

Monica wanted to go to museums. She wanted to attend evening community lectures at the university. She wanted to join a quilting club. She wanted to *do* things.

A sudden realization made her feel the way she felt when she woke up on her birthday. Maybe she *could* start doing all those things.

Monica smiled and then put her hand over her mouth and looked about as if someone might have seen her. Was it a sin to be glad her husband was dead? Well, maybe not glad. But not sad, either. She put the jar of spaghetti sauce back in the cupboard and looked at her watch. There was still just barely time to get to the store and back before Gatlin came home. She could buy fresh Brussels sprouts and asparagus and a salad. She could have what *she* wanted for dinner. She hugged herself and smiled again.

Monica grabbed her purse and headed out the door. Mariano's was only a little over a mile away. She parked as close as she could to the entrance and grabbed a red plastic basket as she went through the doors. She stopped and stared as she entered the produce section. It was truly beautiful. She felt like a girl from Zimbabwe entering a big suburban market for the first time. Raymond of course hated fresh vegetables. If they had any at all, they were canned. Monica swept along the displays, putting items in her basket, hoping none of her neighbors were there to see her expression. What would they think of Mormons if she seemed happy to hear about her husband's death?

Maybe they'd think she had a lot of faith in the Resurrection.

Of course, it was true she'd still be stuck with Raymond in the Celestial Kingdom. But that wouldn't be for a while yet, and at least there'd be no equity loans there. The two of them sometimes watched reruns of *Everybody Loves Raymond*, and Monica would think to herself, "Well, not *everybody*."

She was horrible. Horrible. Maybe she was just in shock. That might be it. She should call the bishop and make an appointment for some counseling. She should pray. She should fast.

Fast. Not prepare a great meal!

At the edge of the produce section were some cut flowers. Monica saw some white Calla lilies and giggled, thinking of Katherine Hepburn. She added them to her basket. Gatlin would think someone had sent them. No one had to know she was buying flowers for herself. She headed to the checkout line, glancing again at her watch.

As she pulled out her credit card, Monica had another thought. Would she be more upset about Raymond's death if she was now poor? Would being upset solely for financial reasons be worse than not being upset now?

She saw *People* magazine with Ben Affleck on the cover. There was also some soap opera digest showing a man with chiseled features. Monica realized she wasn't even interested in dating again, not in the slightest. Her grandfather had died at seventy-five while her grandmother was seventy-three. Gammie was still alive at ninety-one and had never seemed happier than in these last eighteen years.

Did other women like feeling free, too?

Not feeling free, Monica thought. *Being* free. She closed her eyes and inhaled deeply. When the checker called out to her, she smiled apologetically and finished putting her items on the conveyor belt.

Monica could get a part-time job. It didn't matter doing what. She only had one year of college behind her. Maybe she could spend some of that life insurance on tuition for herself. And she'd always wanted to convert the spare bedroom to a studio and start painting. Raymond said it would be a waste of time and money and space. Maybe Monica could take an art class now.

She could be part of the world again.

Swiping her card and entering her pin, Monica frowned. Would that make her worldly?

She picked up her bag of produce and the cut flowers and headed out of the store and back toward her car. She and Raymond and Gatlin had plane tickets to Orlando for a three-day stay next month. Raymond always chose where they'd go on vacation. He always chose the paint colors for the house, the furniture, the movies they'd watch, where they sat in the chapel. He always got his way in everything. Maybe she could exchange the tickets for a trip to New York.

Would Raymond be the one to choose the color of the sky on the planet they created together?

Maybe she could finally paint the bedroom lavender.

It was *her* turn now.

Monica sang along with the radio on the short ride home and brought her purchases into the house. She put the flowers in her best crystal vase and then started rinsing the vegetables. Gatlin should be home from band practice soon. They'd have dinner, and then she'd face the gruesome task of identifying her husband and arranging for the funeral. There'd be no eulogy, though. She didn't want to hear a eulogy.

She looked at one of the stalks of asparagus as she washed and thought about Saturday nights. Neither she nor Raymond liked to give oral sex, so they always just practiced the missionary position, always over in six minutes.

Thank God there'd be no more of that.

She put the asparagus in one steamer and the Brussels sprouts in another.

Maybe she'd sneak downtown someday and buy a vibrator.

Monica heard the door open. There was Gatlin now. She bit her lip hard so that she wouldn't smile when she told him the news.

"Hi, honey, I'm home."

Monica's heart started pounding, and a second later, Raymond walked into the kitchen. "You'll never believe what happened to me today," he began, not giving her a kiss but grabbing a soda out of the fridge. "Some pickpocket stole my wallet. I didn't even realize it until I went to the vending machine at 4:00 to buy a Snickers."

Monica stood staring at the man as he headed for the living room and plopped down on the sofa, kicking off his shoes.

His feet always stank.

"I spent the last hour at work canceling cards. Now I'll have to go in an hour early tomorrow. And sheesh, let me tell you about this one loan. The loan officer has been harping and harping on me to get the appraisal done, and when I do, I find she hasn't even filled out the OFAC Alerts screen yet."

Raymond continued droning on, and Monica looked at her asparagus as if a good friend had just been murdered. She emptied the two steamers, dumping the vegetables into the compost pail. Then she pulled out her big pot and started boiling some water. She took the jar of Newman's back out of the cupboard and wrenched the lid off.

The act exhausted her. She leaned against the counter.

"And *then* she says, 'I don't see why we can't make an exception and give him $50,000 over the guidelines'! It's just pathetic."

"I'm sorry you had such a bad day, dear," Monica said softly. "But you're home now. You relax in front of the TV, and I'll get dinner started."

# Lyeing for the Lord

"Come on, sweetie," said Mirabel. "It's the Sabbath. I don't want to work by cooking a big meal. Let's stop at Eat Up on the way home."

"Doing business on Sunday is a sin, too, honey," Henry replied.

"Sweetie, we've just sat through two hours of stake conference. Surely, we deserve some kind of break."

"Oh, all right. I just hope no one sees us go inside. The Bishop is already on my case for not volunteering at the Bishop's Storehouse last month."

Mirabel smiled. Sometimes, living in Salt Lake, you were expected to be role models for the whole Church. It felt good to break a rule now and then. One of the talks at conference today was on tithing. Brother Cowley, the first counselor in the stake presidency, had told the story of a man who didn't pay his tithing one week, and his car broke down. The repairs ended up costing exactly what his tithing would have been. When the man resumed paying his tithing, his car worked fine. Several months later, when he skipped a payment again, the car broke down once more. The man started calling the vehicle his "tithing car," and he became completely converted to the principle of tithing. He'd been paying regularly for the past three years, and his car hadn't broken down since.

Mirabel hated talks like those. Was she supposed to believe that if the man continued to pay his tithing for the next twenty years, the car would never have any more problems? Or were any future problems related solely to legitimate wear, and not tithing? Mormons could interpret ordinary life events in any way they wanted.

The worst part, though, was that Mirabel actually knew the family in this story. And Brother Cowley got his facts wrong. The first payment repair hadn't cost the exact amount of the tithing payment. It had cost about a third. And the car had continued to have problems even after the family resumed their tithing payments, just not as severe as the first problem. Mormons not only interpreted as they chose, they also rewrote history as they chose. Everyone knew about it. It was called "lying for the Lord." It was perfectly acceptable to tell lies, to break one of God's Ten Commandments, if one did it to promote faith.

The scriptures said that liars would go to the Telestial Kingdom, the lowest degree of heaven. If Church leaders could lie and get away with it, though, what was the harm in going to a restaurant on Sunday? Surely, it was the lesser sin. Especially since she didn't intend to lie about it.

A few minutes later, Mirabel and Henry pulled into the parking lot of Eat Up in Holladay, less than a mile from their home. Henry looked about as if afraid of being seen, but Mirabel felt that the only people close enough to identify her would be others like herself, so she wasn't particularly worried.

A young hostess, sinning by working on the Sabbath, led them to a table. Well, naturally, the girl wouldn't be sinning in the first place if there weren't customers like Mirabel and Henry giving her an incentive to do so. Sometimes, however, especially on conference days, Mirabel wondered if it might be better to do things other than attend church. An hour-long Sacrament meeting was bad enough, but two hours of conference? Wasn't it a sin for the leaders to inflict that much boredom on that many members?

Why could leaders sin all the time without any consequences, while there were always negative consequences for the regular members?

Even Paul H. Dunn, the former apostle, had only had his hand slapped when it turned out he was lying about his baseball and World War II experiences, retooling the actual events until they were overwhelmingly faith promoting. The problem with faith-promoting stories was that they were only faith promoting if they were true. When you had to lie to promote faith, you kind of lost your moral superiority.

"What do you think you're going to have?" asked Henry, looking over the plastic-coated menu.

"I'm thinking a pulled pork sandwich," Mirabel replied. "How about you?"

"Maybe some ribs."

Where was the sin in that? They were just having a pleasant meal, relaxing and enjoying each other's company. Henry wouldn't be able to run off to his office in the basement, and Mirabel wouldn't pick up yet another magazine to read. They'd have at least half an hour of real communication. No sin there. Of course, lots of people these days felt that eating meat was a sin, but the Church didn't condemn it, so Mirabel was certainly not going to feel guilty about it. She had enough sins to worry about. Last week, she'd skipped choir rehearsal. Singing in the choir wasn't a commandment, but if you joined, you were certainly obligated to practice. Sometimes, Mirabel fantasized about auditioning for the Mormon Tabernacle Choir, but she knew she simply wouldn't be able to make all the rehearsals. Even singing, which was delightfully fun, became a chore when it was mandatory. And if it was in any way a Church calling, it automatically became mandatory. Mirabel could always lie and say she was sick, but lying left a bad taste in her mouth and she'd just rather not do it.

"What'll we tell the Halvorsons when we get back to the house late?" asked Henry. "They left church the same time we did."

"Do we have to say anything at all?" Mirabel returned. "They can just wonder and assume what they want. We don't have to answer to them."

"They might say something to someone else."

"So let them."

Mirabel gripped her menu more tightly, bending the plastic. Mormons reported on each other all the time. In other communities, it was called gossip and was a sin. But Mormons felt an obligation to keep each other on the straight and narrow. Such spying was called being a good Latter-day Saint.

"Can I get you anything to drink?" asked another young woman, blond, standing at their table with a bright smile. She was so sweet. She had to be Mormon.

"I'll have a Coke," said Henry.

"I'll have the sweet tea," said Mirabel.

Henry stared at her.

"And are you ready to make your order?" the girl continued. When Mirabel nodded, both she and Henry gave their food orders. Henry stumbled over his words, still shocked by what Mirabel had done.

After the girl walked away, Henry leaned over and hissed, "What do you think you're doing? Breaking the Word of Wisdom on the Sabbath?"

"Would you rather I break it on a weekday?"

Henry frowned. "Why break it at all?"

"Because I like sweet tea."

"And how would you know? You've been Mormon all your life."

Mirabel just smiled.

Maybe it was time to quit the ward choir altogether. And maybe she should resign her position as second counselor in the Relief Society. She didn't *have* to make church the absolute focus of her life every day of the week. She had her three children, and her grandchildren. She had her quilting. She had her gardening. Mirabel had hardly missed a Sunday in thirty years. Heavenly Father could cut her some slack. She'd still attend, but she didn't have to *work* every Sunday she was at church, did she?

"What did you think of Brother Young's talk?" asked Henry, clearly trying to guide Mirabel back to something spiritual.

Mirabel shrugged. "He said God answers every single prayer." She looked for the server to come back with their drinks. "I'm not sure I believe that. I've had lots of prayers go unanswered." Like finding joy at church the way she was supposed to.

"Maybe it was just that the answer was no."

Here came the girl with the drinks. Mirabel decided not to say what she was thinking, that Henry's was a pat answer. If God helped you, he was answering your prayer. If he didn't help you, he was answering your prayer. If things were going well in your life, God was answering your prayer. If things were crap in your life, God was answering your prayer. Basically, you were again just interpreting random events any way you wanted, not looking at the facts.

Maybe Mirabel should consider actually skipping church once in a while, too.

She took a long sip of the sweet tea, and suddenly her mouth and throat were on fire. She spit out what she could and gasped. "I think I've just drank acid!" she shouted. "Take me to the hospital!"

Henry jumped up and helped her to the car. In agony, Mirabel leaned back, crying in misery. God was punishing her for breaking the Sabbath. He was punishing her for breaking the Word of Wisdom. He was punishing her for doubting.

Heavenly Father was a mean son of a bitch.

Mirabel was rushed through the emergency room, where it was discovered she had severe burns in her mouth and esophagus, the result of ingesting lye. She was admitted to the ICU in critical condition. The next few days, she lingered between life and death, asleep most of the time, though continually moaning in pain.

Finally, late on the third day, she seemed to start improving just a bit. "What happened?" she asked Henry weakly. She was vaguely aware that he'd been by her side the entire time.

"It was some kid at the restaurant named Jared," Henry replied haltingly, putting his hand on hers. "A priest from our own ward."

"Wh-what did he do?" It hurt to talk.

"He deliberately put a powdered degreaser into the tea. He wanted to teach people that drinking tea was wrong."

Mirabel shook her head against the pillow and started crying. It made her throat hurt more.

"That's not out in the news, though," Henry continued. "The bishop is keeping it quiet, having the kid tell everyone it was just an accident, a mistake. He doesn't want the Church to look bad. And Jared is really a good kid."

"*I'll* tell," whispered Mirabel. "*I'll* tell."

"Oh, honey, you can't. The bishop will come and explain it later. We've got to do the right thing."

Mirabel said nothing but tried to relax. Even with the pain medication, she felt miserable. Lying was so caustic, she thought, and wasn't that what the Church did all the time? She heard rumors about all the lies the leaders told about Church history. For the first time, she began to wonder if the Church itself was a lie. What if Joseph Smith wasn't a prophet? What if

President Monson wasn't a prophet? What if the Book of Mormon was just a book?

Her cousin Allen was gay. Mirabel remembered the shock she felt when he divorced his wife of sixteen years, saying he'd lived his whole life as a lie. For the first time, she understood what he meant.

Mirabel decided she wasn't going back to church at all anymore. She'd join a community chorus, one that didn't make singing feel like a payment which had to be made, and—

What if she were never able to sing anymore?

She started crying again and Henry squeezed her hand. She could feel the tape where the IV was attached twisting under the pressure. Henry leaned toward her and whispered soothingly in her ear. "It'll be okay, honey," he said. "It'll be okay."

Lies, lies, lies, thought Mirabel. Everything was lies. If she got better, she was going to the grocery and buy a two-liter bottle of sweet tea. And she would tell everyone what she was drinking.

Mirabel looked over at Henry, whose face was contorted with pain. His love wasn't a lie, anyway. That was something. She'd have to make more of an effort to spend time with him.

Would he still love her after she left the Church?

"It'll be okay, honey," he whispered again, patting her arm.

It will be after I speak to a reporter, she thought.

Mirabel closed her eyes, her eyelids heavy with all the medication, and drifted painfully back to sleep. Just before she lost consciousness, Mirabel could hear Henry on the phone asking the bishop to come talk to her. Not to give her a blessing, she realized, but only to convince her to stay quiet. Then again, she may have received a blessing earlier when she was first admitted and just didn't remember it. If she recovered, she'd probably become the bishop's new faith-promoting story of Heavenly Father's mercy and forgiveness. She tried to envision the scene as she put the bishop witheringly in his place, but after a moment, she could see nothing at all.

# A Tithing of Queers

–

Back when I was in the Church, I held almost every calling imaginable. I taught early morning Seminary. I taught Sunday school. I taught the Teachers' Quorum. I taught the Elders' Quorum. I was Single Adult rep for my ward. I was Single Adult chair for the stake. I was a Home Teacher (who wasn't?). Some of the callings I didn't care for, but some of them were okay. The point is that I was serving others whether I liked it or not. The Church downright forced active members to behave unselfishly.

If you could say that serving in those callings simply so we'd have a better shot of making it to the Celestial Kingdom was an unselfish motive.

Now that I had left the Church, though, I found that I didn't do much volunteer work. I used to help clean up after the AIDS Walk once a year, but then the organizers started getting prison inmates to do it. I used to help out at the Sierra Club once a month, but driving up to Shoreline and back soon became too much trouble. I signed petitions when they came in my email, until I ended up with a virus once by clicking the wrong thing.

What could I do to make myself help others more?

I had a friend in AA who did lots of service work, but I didn't want to become an alcoholic just so I could work on my altruism. The few friends I had who attended different religious services told me their clergy and religion teachers were paid for their work. Not much volunteering in their places of worship. They even hired their janitors. Imagine.

There wasn't much left to try.

I did mow my neighbor's yard for a while. They were a young married couple who always let their grass grow too high, but after a while, the husband felt embarrassed by my help and started hiring it out.

I used to pay tithing while still a Mormon, and even now, four years after I'd left the Church, I still paid ten percent of my income to various causes. That made me feel a *little* generous, but writing a check to the Perkins School for the Blind wasn't the same as actually helping a blind person do their grocery shopping. You had to be directly involved to feel truly good about yourself.

Feeling good about myself was a selfish motive, of course, not an altruistic one. The real reason I needed to be directly involved was in order to legitimately grow as a person.

Or was personal growth selfish, too?

I knew I could always volunteer at a soup kitchen, but that didn't sound very appealing. And I didn't want to help clean up parks. Or tutor illiterate children. I was selfish. That was the whole problem I was trying to address. But how did one stop being selfish long enough to do the things which would help him stop being selfish?

"Brett," said my friend George, calling me on my cell. It was Saturday morning, around 10:15. "We're really short-handed today down at Lifelong AIDS. We need some help preparing food."

Sounded unpleasant. George had asked me to help before and I'd always turned him down. But how could I pretend to be honestly seeking self-improvement if I did so now? "I'll be there in half an hour," I replied.

"You're the best."

No, I wasn't. But I drove over to Capitol Hill from my home in south Seattle and went inside the office. There a man named Damian walked me to another nearby building, and I joined a couple of older women and got to work. We spent half an hour breaking apart frozen chicken breasts and putting two in each plastic bag, tying each bag off with a tie. My hands were frozen by the time we finished. And there was no chatting, other than handing things off to each other.

After this, we took big containers of rice and poured a set amount into other plastic bags and tied them off. This took another half hour. We followed that by opening large brown paper grocery bags and putting bags of rice in each one, then boxes of almond milk in each, then boxes of cereal in each, then cans of vegetables and cans of fruit in each, followed by a couple of other items I forget now.

George was in some other area packaging several different items. I didn't see him till I'd been there over three hours. By that time, I was ready to go home.

"That wasn't so bad, was it?" asked George, patting me on the back.

I thought of the times I'd helped out at the Bishop's Storehouse, doing essentially the same thing. Somehow, that had felt edifying, helping poor Mormons, but helping poor people with HIV and AIDS didn't feel as rewarding.

Why was that, I wondered? Something must be wrong with me.

The Church *endorsed* all its service imperatives. When I did some kind of service back at church, I knew I was building my Celestial resumé. When I did it now, with no thought of the afterlife, helping out just felt like work.

But if I was irritated with the Church for building its own empire and ignoring the needy of the world, why didn't I want to actually help those needy people now that I had a chance?

Well, it was boring.

"Sure, George," I replied. "I'll have to come back again sometime."

"How about next week?"

I shook my head. "Too soon."

"Poor people are hungry around the clock, you know."

Ah, there it was—guilt. Something I could relate to. But George couldn't send me to hell for refusing to give in to it, the way my bishop and stake president could.

"I'll see what my schedule is like."

"Okay, Brett, okay."

After leaving Lifelong, I was feeling too melancholy to head straight back home. It was after 2:00, and I was hungry, so I left my truck parked near Madison and headed to Broadway. I saw a man begging in front of the QFC grocery and ignored him. I continued walking, past the community college and toward

Rosa's, a tiny pizzeria I liked. I bought a slice of pepperoni and a slice of cheese pizza and sat at a little table on the sidewalk.

A girl with spiky blond hair and three nose rings walked by with her pit bull on a leash. I watched as she asked a woman around thirty for change. The woman said no.

After I finished eating, I walked up to Volunteer Park, an ironic place, I mused, to mull over my dilemma. I sat on a bench overlooking the greenhouse and reflected a long while. Sometimes, I thought about going back to church, even if they wouldn't baptize me, and trying to accept a calling, only I knew the leaders would never let me have a calling if I wasn't a member.

Perhaps I could be celibate for just a couple of years so I could be rebaptized and have another calling long enough to finally internalize the principle of service.

Only I couldn't go a week without picking someone up at a bar.

Why couldn't I volunteer with Jewish Family Services and help an old man clean his apartment? Why couldn't I volunteer with Catholic Charities and help an immigrant learn English? Why couldn't I volunteer at a Boys Club and help some young kid learn to throw a ball?

I did know how to throw a ball.

I watched a young woman enter the greenhouse across the lawn from me.

I *could* help people in any number of ways. I knew that. I just didn't *want* to.

The Church used to make me be good. How could I make myself do it alone?

Well, I often had sex with old, fat men. My father hadn't been fat. Neither had either grandfather. And no favorite bishop or mission president, either, for that matter, so I didn't know why old, fat guys turned me on. But they were plentiful, and they seemed to like my firm twenty-eight-year-old body just fine.

Was *that* volunteer work?

I was also a good listener in bars, as people of all ages unloaded on me. Several people told me I seemed like a priest, and they told me all their deepest secrets, even while trying to pick me up. Believe me, hearing about the time a guy killed his neighbor's dog because it barked too much was not the thing to get me in the mood. But I listened. Sometimes, that's all the men needed. Other times, they wanted advice, and I practiced being Dear Abby.

Gays were less damaged these days than they'd been in the past. Even with all my religious baggage, coming out couldn't have been as hard for me as for guys back in the 1960's. But some of them still needed a general kind of love that was neither platonic nor sexual, and I could give that easily enough.

Yet that wasn't enough of a contribution to the world.

I'd always wanted to join the Seattle Men's Chorus, I realized, but had just never gotten around to it. Maybe I could do that now. Helping create a positive image of gay men was a good thing, wasn't it? Yet, if I enjoyed what I was doing, it wasn't much of a sacrifice.

Did doing good have to be a sacrifice?

I went online and found out the time and place for the next rehearsal and put it on my calendar. Then I stared at the people slowly walking by, oblivious and happy. I eventually grew tired of sitting and walked over to the greenhouse. It was hot and humid inside, filled with exotic plants. Even though workers were paid to care for these plants, I thought, they were still doing a good deed, making the world a better place. Perhaps one didn't have to do it for free to be making a real contribution.

Doctors and nurses and teachers and farmers made real contributions.

I worked as a carpenter, doing small remodeling jobs. Sure, my clients were grateful for the help I gave them, and I did convert many old, run-down, ill-conceived bathrooms and kitchens into useful and productive and happy places. But was that enough of an addition to the planet? Didn't I have to convert a million people from the political right to the political left? Didn't I have to stop global warming?

It was just maddening. It was so much easier when I could settle all these worries simply by teaching my assigned family a Home Teaching lesson.

I went back to the bench and sat until it grew dark around 6:00. After a while, I walked slowly back to my truck. I passed another man begging in front of the QFC, and this time, I gave him a quarter. Then I felt like a heel for not giving more.

Driving home, I thought about what I was trying to do. Maybe it was enough to be a good citizen and vote for good candidates and pay my taxes. Maybe I didn't *have* to do fifteen hours of volunteer work a week. Maybe it was okay just to be nice to the people I came in contact with every day. If guilt was the only thing pushing me to be Superman, I wasn't sure my motivation was all that impressive to begin with.

I was taking the back roads to avoid the freeway and was now entering the Central District. It was a traditionally black neighborhood but had started gentrifying several years ago. Some parts were still poor and run-down, and other parts were up and coming. I approached a convenience store and saw a young woman with her hand outstretched in the standard hitchhiking signal. She looked a little tarty, with a short skirt and high heels, but not dangerous. I figured she'd just gotten dumped by a boyfriend while on a date and needed a ride home.

I pulled into the parking lot. Before I even waved her over, she approached the truck. "Where you headed?" she asked. She had unnaturally large breasts. At least they seemed so in the tight blouse she was wearing.

"I'm driving to Rainier Beach. Where do you need to go?" I noticed now that the woman was wearing extraordinarily heavy make-up. She looked like a tramp. But I wasn't here to judge. She was a person in need, and I had the ability to help. That's what this was all about.

"Columbia City," she replied. That was another area in transition.

"Hop on in." Maybe all I really needed to do was be responsive to the people I came in contact with on a daily basis, not go out of my way to find organized ways to serve.

She opened the passenger door and slid into the seat, and I pulled back out onto Martin Luther King. I didn't try to engage the woman in conversation. I didn't have to know why she needed a ride. She didn't seem to feel the need to ask why I had picked her up, either.

About ten minutes later, though, as we were driving down Rainier Avenue, she reached into her purse and pulled out a tiny gun. "Give me all your money," she said calmly.

"What?"

"You heard me. How much you got?"

"I'm not giving you any money." Was this a test, I wondered? And if it were, was it a test from God or a test from the devil? I wasn't sure I even believed in either anymore. There were simply occasional unwanted consequences to any action.

Even good deeds.

But one didn't do them because one was always rewarded. One did them because they were the right thing to do.

Wasn't that the correct answer?

"I'll shoot you."

I felt so disappointed with her and with myself as well that I didn't even feel alarmed. "No, you won't," I said evenly. "I'll just drive to the nearest police station and let you off there." Maybe there was something to be said for that organized helping, after all, rather than picking up strays on the street.

The woman laughed. "You do, and I'll tell them you picked up a known prostitute and refused to pay her. I'll get arrested, but that's no big deal for me. You'll be arrested, too. All your friends will hear."

"My friends know I'm gay and would never pick up a prostitute." I'd never even picked up a cheap hustler. Of course, friends were always quick to assume the worst, so who knew how they'd really react. Maybe it was best to pay her. I only had $40 in my wallet. It wouldn't be a terrible loss.

"Your boss will find out."

"I'm self-employed." I realized suddenly that despite the provocation, not only did I not feel alarmed, but I also didn't feel any anger toward this woman, only sadness.

But that was hardly going to help her in any meaningful way.

The woman lifted the gun and directed it closer to my head. "Give me your money."

"I have friends in AA and NA who can help you if you need it."

"Aw, man…"

I pulled into the brightly lit parking lot of a Rite Aid. "Why don't I let you off here?" I suggested. I hoped the lights would weaken her desire to do bad things.

"Give me your money or I'll shoot out your tires."

"What good will that do you?"

The woman put her gun back in her purse. "Man, you are one fucking pain in the ass." She jumped out of the truck and slammed the door.

I had the oddest desire to ask her if she wanted me to send the sister missionaries to her place.

I resisted the impulse and pulled back onto Rainier. I didn't pick anyone else up on the way home.

But as I was still feeling a little down, I stopped at the Safeway in Rainier Beach to get some ice cream. A nice one and a quarter gallon container of vanilla. There was another man begging in front of this store, too, and I gave him a dollar.

Whatever.

I started to walk away with my ice cream and then turned back.

"What one thing could I buy you in there that would be a real treat for you?" I asked.

"Huh?"

"I can only afford to buy you one thing. What one thing would you like to take home with you tonight?"

The man looked at me suspiciously and then said, "A thick steak."

My prejudices had me expecting him to say alcohol of some type, and I chided myself for that. "I'll be right back," I said and went back into the store. I came out several minutes later with the best steak I could find, though the selection was never great in this one more economically mixed neighborhood. I handed the steak in a paper bag to the man and said, "Enjoy," and got back in my truck.

I wasn't going to be good at organized giving. I just wasn't. But I could still do occasional, unrelated, random acts of kindness. I could do that. Though I suppose it would never truly feel like enough.

I had made such a good Mormon, I thought. Why did God have to make me gay and get me kicked out?

Was it a coincidence that ten percent of the population was gay? Was it God's way of tithing his own Church members, giving away ten percent of his own people? He was giving us to the world, as a gift perhaps, or maybe as a required payment of some sort. Was there something I could do as a non-Mormon, as a gay man, that I couldn't do as a Stepford Husband Latter-day Saint?

Well, I did donate to Single-payer healthcare reform. I donated to candidates who believed in federal work projects to employ the poor and develop infrastructure. I donated to candidates who weren't war hawks. And I voted for politicians who believed in women's healthcare. I saw the world differently as a non-Mormon. Perhaps that was the point of being tithed.

And maybe the fact that volunteering on my own required more effort than having it all decided by my bishop was a good thing.

There was a rally in front of one of the police precincts tomorrow, to protest the fatal shooting by a police officer of an unarmed black man a couple of days ago. I could go to that for half an hour or so. A perfectly respectful tribute to human dignity and human rights that probably not a single active Mormon in the city was going to attend.

I drove back home, ate a salmon fillet, and took a shower. After a brief nap, I brushed my teeth, gargled with mouthwash, and put a condom in my pocket. I climbed back in my truck and made the trip back to Capitol Hill, heading for the bars.

# The Entomology of Words

"So where are we going, Callen?" I asked my husband as he ushered me outside in my best Sunday dress. He was wearing his nicest blue suit. It was our twentieth anniversary, and I knew he'd planned something special.

"Don't worry about a thing, Stephanie. I'll be your valise tonight."

I'd long since given up trying to correct Callen when he used the wrong word. Just now, he was wrong on two counts. First, the word he was trying for was valet, and second, the word he needed to be trying for was chauffeur. At first, his mistakes had seemed endearing, but over the years, they'd almost become infuriating. I'd even asked Callen once to get a blessing from our Home Teachers to heal him. When that didn't work, I asked for blessings from our bishop and then from our stake president. Nothing changed.

Callen then suggested that *I* get a blessing so that I wouldn't be as bothered by the misfiring of his brain sinuses.

I began to wonder if he really did have sinuses in his brain instead of synapses.

I couldn't put my finger on just *why* these errors annoyed me so. Everyone else found them funny. I wondered if I was simply being unreasonable. But I really didn't think so. I gave up my job as an elementary school teacher when we got married so I could be an appropriate wife and mother. I learned all of Callen's favorite foods and practiced different recipes so that he was always satisfied. I kept the house clean. I was Nursery leader. I was Beehive instructor. I was even first counselor in the Relief Society at one point. And I raised three beautiful children, John, Stacy, and Caroline. John would be leaving on his mission in another two months. Stacy was sixteen and Caroline fourteen. I'd taught each of them to read by the time they were four, and they were all great students. None of them had Callen's problem with malapropisms.

Thank goodness for that.

Callen drove for about twenty minutes, and we finally pulled up to an elegant seafood restaurant on the waterfront of Lake Union. It was where we'd celebrated our fifth, tenth, and fifteenth anniversaries as well. "I love Ralph's," I said, smiling. "Thank you."

"I know how much you like those scarabs," he said, grinning. Indeed, scallops were my very favorite seafood.

We parked the car about a block from the restaurant so that we wouldn't have to pay for parking, and we walked in the summery, cool breeze up to the front door. Callen opened it for me, and we stepped inside. There, a young girl took our names and led us to a table by a window. Callen had actually thought ahead to make a reservation, I realized, something he hadn't done the previous three times we'd come here.

Callen had a low-level office job in downtown Seattle and didn't bring home much money, yet he'd always forbidden me to return to work, so we didn't splurge like this often. We usually went someplace like Denny's on our other anniversaries. Would an evening at a nice restaurant be less impressive if it were ordinary? I wished we could eat here once a month. But we were a "faithful" Latter-day Saint family, Callen insisted. "We follow God's ordained gender rolls."

Not a malapropism orally, but that was the way he wrote it, too.

Sometimes, when Callen said "faith," I still thought he was using the wrong word. Faith was more than a belief. One could believe in the Easter Bunny, after all. Faith was a belief in things that were true. But lately, I wasn't sure we really *knew* that. For me, faith was a belief in things I hoped were true. That wasn't quite the same thing. We always bore our testimony that we "knew" the Church was true, but "know" really only meant "I *want* it to be true."

"I really have an infinity for the cooking here," said Callen, inspecting his menu. "You do a great job, of course, but it's always nice to try someone else's cooking once in a while." He'd admitted to me years ago that he looked forward to the Celestial Kingdom when he could start "cooking" with other women. *He'd* get variety for eternity. I'd still be stuck with the same man.

But maybe in heaven he'd at least speak correctly.

"Ah, poached salmon with holiday sauce." He sighed.

How could he get the word wrong when he was looking right at it?

The server came to the table a few minutes later, and Callen ordered for both of us. He didn't ask me what I wanted, knowing already I'd pick the scallops. I didn't particularly mind, though part of me would still have liked to be asked. He ordered Diet 7-Up for us both. I would have preferred a regular Coke, but I could only have those on the rare occasions when I went out for lunch by myself. Even though the Church had stated publicly it didn't condemn cola drinks, Callen was sure this position was only PR, that secretly God still forbade it. The Church was trying to become more "mainstream," which actually mean "ordinary." If you didn't stand out, if you weren't special, what was the point of being Mormon?

"How was your day, dear?" asked Callen, looking out the window at the boats near the jetty. The early evening sunshine flickered on the waves.

I thought about how to answer Callen's question. Today was a Thursday, which meant it was pretty much like a Wednesday. Or a Tuesday. I forced myself to find something to say. "John is still not speaking to Caroline."

"Why not?"

"Because of what she did to him last weekend when they were sunbathing."

"And what was that?" asked Callen.

I smiled. Both children had argued about it at the table right in front of Callen last Saturday. He could be quite oblivious when he wanted to be.

Like he was when he forgot my birthday two months ago.

"While John was sleeping on his stomach, Caroline wrote 'Wash Me' on his back in sunscreen. By the time he woke up, he was tanned everywhere except where she'd written. Now he can't play basketball without his shirt."

"He'll soon be wearing garments and not have to worry about that kind of nonsense anymore."

"Well, he's worrying about it now."

Soon our meals arrived. At these fancy restaurants, the entrée was always small, so I began taking very tiny bites and savoring each one. I had finished talking about my day—there wasn't much to say—and now Callen was eager to tell me about his. "I have several funny antidotes from work," he said. "The first one has a little double entawdry."

I gritted my teeth as Callen happily told me about his day. *Why* wasn't I eager to hear about it, I wondered? Being a stay-at-home Mom was so boring I should jump at the chance to hear of other activities. And yet somehow it was like pouring salt on a wound. While I knew I had the world's best job, at times I had to admit I felt suffocated. "World's best job" seemed to be the wrong word choice, too. Perhaps a better term would be "world's most primitive job." If cavewomen were doing this 20,000 years ago, what was the point of evolution?

And if mothering were all I'd be doing in heaven, what was the point of becoming a god?

"Isn't that a write-up?" asked Callen, finishing a story and slapping the table.

"Yes, quite a riot," I replied. I had no idea what he'd been talking about.

The kids were almost grown. Even the girls had little use for me these days, in that stage where mothers don't know anything. I knew Callen had sacrificed for this nice meal to celebrate our anniversary, but I wondered if I could dare ask him for what I truly wanted.

He recounted another anecdote and I smiled dutifully.

He ate the last bite of his salmon, and I had the last of my scallops. I was still hungry, but that was okay. It had still been a lovely meal.

"It's a special day," said Callen. "Want some dessert? I see they have sconces on the menu."

"No, I'm good," I said quietly.

"Oh, live a little, Stephanie. Spontanuity is a good thing."

I smiled again and shook my head while Callen ordered a scoop of ice cream with caramel sauce.

"Oh, I don't want to leave," I said as he finished his last mouthful. "It's so lovely here." I looked at the boats on the lake. We'd be back again in just five more years, I thought.

"I still have a little surprise for you when we get home." Callen smiled.

It was no surprise what he'd be doing once we were home.

He paid the check, we walked back to the car, and we drove back home to Shoreline slowly. The kids were all in their rooms, and Callen and I went to ours and changed out of our nice clothes. I put on my best nightgown, but it was hard to feel terribly sexy while wearing Mormon underwear. Callen put on his striped pajamas. Now it was time for me to give my husband *his* gift. It was always the same every year. He loved entering me from behind. I hated it and only allowed it on our anniversary. When I lay on my stomach and spread my flap, he always giggled and called me his "sex toy."

He never got that word wrong.

The look Callen was giving me now told me he was in the mood for his gift right away. But I still wanted to talk to him first. If I couldn't do it now, it would never get done.

"Sweetheart," I began.

"Yes?"

"I really loved your present this year."

"Thank you."

"But I was wondering if I could ask for something else, too."

Callen frowned.

"What I'd really like to do is work in a restaurant myself. I've made out a short resumé, and I'd like to start applying for jobs this week."

Callen stared at me.

"If you think it's okay."

Callen took a deep breath and looked down at the floor. "Well, I don't know…" he said slowly.

"I'm a great cook. You said so yourself. Can you take a look at my resumé tomorrow and see if it looks alright?"

Callen continued staring at the floor.

"Please?"

Callen sighed. "I suppose so. I'll give it a cursive look in the morning. But I'll want you to talk to the bishop about this on Sunday."

I already knew what the bishop would say, of course. The teenage years were especially hard on girls, and I needed to be available to them 24/7, the way Heavenly Father intended. I gritted my teeth again. *I* was a malapropism, I realized. When people called me a wife and mother, they didn't mean "person."

"Come on, dear," I said, lying down on the bed and lifting my nightgown up. "I'll recite all the prophets and the current General Authorities while you get to work. You always like that." I only recited names on our anniversary. It made him feel that what he was doing to me wasn't as nasty as it actually was, if we could turn it into a religious exercise as well.

He grinned and opened his fly. "I don't know how you remember all those names in order," he said. "You and your pneumatic devices."

I was face down on the bed now and heard him applying lotion to his penis. He entered me and groaned in pleasure. I was glad he couldn't see my scowl. But I put a smile in my voice as I said, "I'll start applying for jobs in the morning, sweetheart. It'll help pay for the girls' mission funds."

Callen grunted and pushed himself in harder.

"Joseph Smith," I began. "Brigham Young. John Taylor. Wilford Woodruff. Lorenzo Snow…."

"Honey, you're the best wife a man could ever have." He shoved harder and harder.

I smiled tightly against the mattress. I wasn't going to talk to the bishop. And I'd get a professional to evaluate my resumé. Starting tomorrow, I wouldn't be a malapropism any more.

"Joseph F. Smith!" I shouted. "Heber J. Grant!"

"Oh, honey, I love you!"

There he was, still misusing words, I thought. He was such a...such a... schmutz. Ha! But I'd stay with him in the Celestial Kingdom anyway.

And I wouldn't let him have any more wives.

Well, maybe just one—a former Laurel instructor, perhaps, or Relief Society president, who liked taking it from behind.

# Trapped in a Vagina

"My Dad told me that during the Viet Nam war, some prostitutes would put razor blades in their vagina, and when a serviceman would enter her, his penis would get cut in half." Elder Blake, our district leader here in Tübingen, Germany, said this casually as we sat around the dinner table in our tiny missionary apartment.

"Ooh, gross!" said my senior companion, Elder Myre, but he was laughing.

"I had a friend in high school who was dating a cheerleader," said Elder Johnson, the DL's companion. "They had a fight and were having make-up sex, and when she went down on him, she bit off his dick."

Everyone gasped in horror but giggled, too.

"Even when girls aren't up to something nefarious," Elder Blake continued, "you still don't know what you're getting yourself in for. She could have cooties in there. You're blindly submitting yourself to who knows what every time you go in. That's why it's so important to marry someone pure."

As Mormon missionaries, not even allowed to masturbate for the two years we'd be out here serving the Lord, our dinner conversation often turned to sex. All four of us were virgins, of course, but most of the guys, especially Elder Blake, always tried to sound as if they knew what they were talking about. I hoped they did, because this was about the extent of my sexual education.

"What about you, Elder Schneider?" asked Elder Blake, pointing at me. "What warnings have you heard?"

"I read an article about a woman who inserted a mouse trap in her vagina," I said.

"Ooh!"

I'd heard no such thing, naturally, and didn't even know if it was physically possible, but I wanted to be part of the conversation.

"I saw a news show," said Elder Johnson, "where this woman cut off her husband's dick after they had sex and he fell asleep. She drove away and threw it out a window. But a neighbor found it and the doctors were able to sew it back on. The guy eventually became a porn star."

"No way!"

Our talk continued for the rest of the meal. I was always on the lookout for faith-promoting stories, not so I could tell them to investigators here, but so I could tell my family and friends back home. I knew Europe was a tough mission field for baptisms, but my mother had included a letter with my mission papers insisting I be sent somewhere "civilized." As a result, I didn't expect to climb down into the baptismal font very often, but I hoped I could at least help those I loved who were already in the Church become stronger in their faith. Yet with so much of our talk centered on sex, I didn't feel inspired most of the time. "Please, Heavenly Father," I prayed silently, "help me help other Mormons." It was great for all us missionaries to bring in a couple of hundred thousand converts a year worldwide, but what point was there to it if we couldn't keep those people in the Church?

After we finished eating, it was my turn to wash dishes, so everyone else scattered to their rooms, afraid I might ask for help. We ate early so that we could still accomplish a decent amount of work in the evenings. Usually, we tried to make appointments with other church members, hoping to "cultivate" them and get them to offer up their friends as investigators. Not many of them cooperated, however, but spending an hour with member families still counted as work time, even if we often got to eat some strudel in the bargain. And again, even if it didn't result in new baptisms, I felt sure our company helped the local members grow stronger.

Tonight, however, Elder Myre and I were giving a talk at the local university, where we hoped to have at least fifty students in attendance. Elder Myre being senior would do most of the speaking. He'd handle most of the questions, too. He didn't actually know any more than I did about the Church. He just thought he did. But I was happy to defer. At least the Church wasn't asking us to stand up on street corners on top of soap boxes like the early missionaries had to do. That kind of thing took balls. Most of our work was pretty routine, if boring. Our numbers reflected that, of course. I'd been out six months and hadn't yet baptized anyone. Elder Myre had been out fourteen and had baptized just one person, an old man who had since died. But he was still a Mormon up in heaven, so I guess it still counted.

The Church had recently lowered the age to begin missionary work from nineteen to eighteen for men, so I didn't even have a year of college behind me the way former missionaries did. I'd gone to the Missionary Training Center three months after graduating high school. Because there'd really been no need for me to get a driver's license at a younger age, I didn't even get that until two months before my mission. I hoped I still remembered how to drive when I got back home.

A man last week had accused us of being too young and inexperienced to "know" the truth, but I'd told him that "out of the mouths of babes" would come wisdom. He replied haughtily, "I'm not going to live my life based on what some kindergarteners say."

"Our prophet is eighty-seven," I said. "Will you listen to *him*?"

The man walked away. Wisdom was wisdom, I thought, no matter where it came from.

I finished the last of the dishes and joined Elder Myre in our room. He was moving his lips as he looked at some notes. "Excited about tonight?" I asked.

He put his papers down and looked at me seriously. "Elder Schneider, we need to set a goal to get at least four new contacts from this meeting."

"Four?" I asked. It seemed unrealistic. Even getting just one would make a good story to tell my family.

"You think five shows more faith?" he asked.

"Oh, four shows plenty of faith," I returned.

"Let's commit ourselves in prayer." Elder Myre got down on his knees and I reluctantly joined him. While I wanted great and exciting things to happen to us, the truth is that I was forced every week in my emails home to significantly stretch events to make them sound even moderately exciting. "We knocked on this door, and the woman who answered turned us away, and then after she closed her door, I heard her sneeze. The Lord was punishing her by making her sick." The truth was she might have already had a cold for three days before we ever knocked. Still, I never lied when I told my stories. I simply made selective edits. But after six months of such efforts, I was beginning to wonder if there were any miracles to talk about any more at all, if there were any truly faith-promoting stories in the first place. I'd read several books filled with them before my mission, and I didn't want to think they were exaggerations. I wanted to believe, but the drought of positive experiences was leaving me feeling parched.

Elder Myre led the prayer, and then we stood up. We put our suit jackets on, shoved our scriptures and some pamphlets in our backpacks, and grabbed our bikes in the hallway. It was early March, but as we were in southern Germany, the weather wasn't too bad. We said goodbye to the other elders and headed out the door.

I liked bicycling. It was too hard to hold a conversation with the wind rushing past our faces, so it was usually a peaceful time. We rode our bikes or took a bus and walked most everywhere we went. I wanted to still be in good shape when I went home to my girlfriend in another eighteen months. Cheryl and I had not even French kissed yet, wanting to save that for after we were married. She'd be seventeen in a few months, almost nineteen by the time I finished my mission. The Church encouraged elders to marry almost as soon as they returned home, afraid we'd fall into sexual sin if we didn't. I wasn't sure I wanted to marry with six years of college still ahead of me, but a commandment was a commandment. God would provide a way for us to get by.

I'd read faith-promoting stories telling me so.

We pulled up onto the campus and chained our bikes to a rack. It was already dark, but the campus was well-lit. "I'd love to study at a place like this," said Elder Myre.

"Won't you?" I asked. Brigham Young was huge and impressive, with the motto, "The world is our campus."

He shook his head. "I'm not going to BYU," he replied. "I already know enough about the Church. They just coddle you there anyway. And they monitor everything you say."

"Shouldn't they?"

"It's like being home-schooled by your mother."

I frowned.

"I'm going to be a mechanic. I already know tons about engines. Been working with my Dad for years. I'll take a few courses at a community college and then join my father's team full-time."

"Well, that sounds fine. Don't you want to do that?"

Elder Myre shrugged. "I like it well enough. But I'd really prefer to *know* something about the world."

"You know German."

"And I'd like to know French, Italian, Spanish, and Dutch, too."

All I wanted to study was Church history. Maybe work for the Church Educational System. Be an Institute teacher somewhere in the mission field helping young adults stay strong in the Church. It used to be that the teenage years were hardest on members. Now it was worst on members in their twenties. While I enjoyed missionary work for the most part, I thought I'd really be better at retention than baptisms. I could teach people how to avoid the temptation of browsing the Internet for false information about the Church, information vulnerable young adults were all too willing to believe. I could fortify them. Since all I was allowed to read as a missionary were Church publications, I saw the benefit of selecting carefully which information made it into one's head.

But I didn't only want to tell *other* people's great stories. I wanted some of my own. Personal stories always carried more weight.

Elder Myre and I walked slowly along the manicured paths. We were a little early and could take our time getting to the auditorium. As we passed a stone sculpture in front of the Microbiology and Virology building, Elder Myre pointed. "What in the world is that?" he asked, laughing. "Abstract art?"

It was a large stone sculpture with a crack in the middle that kind of looked like a river, a canyon tipped vertically. I walked over and read the placard beside it. "It's called Chacàn-Pi," I said. "It means 'Making Love.' It was done by some Peruvian artist." Realization dawned on me and I added, "I think it's supposed to be a vagina."

"A vagina?"

"It says it's the gateway to the world."

Elder Myre laughed. He took out his cell phone and handed it to me. "Take a picture of me in the vagina," he said.

"Do you think that's wise? We could get in trouble."

"Oh, live dangerously, Elder Schneider."

He put his backpack down and stepped inside the tiny crack, putting his face against the lip. I snapped a picture of his wide grin.

"Come on," I said. "Let's get to our meeting."

Elder Myre started to exit but then tripped and fell right on his face. "Ow! Damn!" he said.

"I'll help you." I offered my hand and pulled, but Elder Myre didn't budge.

"My feet are stuck."

I looked at the bottom of the sculpture, where the opening narrowed. Elder Myre's feet were wedged tightly. I pulled on his pants legs but couldn't move him. I pulled harder. Nothing. A couple of other students walked by and snickered. I debated whether or not to ask them for help. What were we going to do?

"We need to pray," Elder Myre said calmly. "Heavenly Father will save us."

We both prayed silently, not wanting to attract any more attention than we already had. "Should I go buy some cooking oil or something?" I asked a moment later. "Some kind of lubricant?" I tugged on his legs again.

"I think you're going to need to call the fire department," Elder Myre said dejectedly.

"Then everyone will know," I protested.

"Look around you." There were already about ten people gathered around us, taking pictures on their cell phones and laughing.

I went up to one of the students and asked, "Could you call the fire department?" I could have done it myself, only I couldn't remember how to call them in Germany. It wasn't 9-1-1. Was it 1-1-2? Or was that for an ambulance? Maybe it was 1-1-0. But wasn't that the police? What was the flippin' number for the fire department?

A pretty blond student had pity on us and made the call, and about fifteen minutes later the first firefighters showed up. By now, a crowd of about twenty students had gathered to watch. "At least it's too dark out here for everyone to see me blush," Elder Myre muttered.

That didn't remain the case for long, as the firefighters beamed a bright light right at the vagina. They used some foam but still couldn't extract my companion. "Should I call Elder Blake?" I asked.

"For heaven's sake, no!" Elder Myre shook his head in misery. Then he sighed heavily, hugged himself, and mumbled softly under his breath, "I want my mama." I thought he might be joking, but he wasn't smiling.

More firefighters came over the next half hour, a total of twenty-three in all. We could hear them talking about the "dumb American" and making other insulting comments. There must have been at least a hundred students gathered around by this time, laughing and pointing and posting pictures online. "I wish I were dead," said Elder Myre.

Then it dawned on me. "This is a test," I said. "You should give your talk to *this* crowd."

"Are you kidding me?"

"No. Do it, Elder!"

It took a few more minutes of convincing, but soon Elder Myre was speaking at the top of his lungs about Joseph Smith and the Book of Mormon and the restoration of the priesthood. This actually encouraged several of the bystanders to leave. Not as good as converting them, but considering the situation, not a bad second choice. Fifteen minutes into Elder Myre's speech, the firefighters finally freed him and he stood up on wobbly feet.

"You won't do anything that stupid again, will you?" asked one of the firefighters, tousling my companion's hair as if he were a little boy.

Elder Myre shook his head quietly.

The firefighters gathered their equipment and headed off, and we were left standing by the vagina with a good eighty students still staring at us. I looked at Elder Myre and nodded. He took a deep breath and continued his talk. When he finished, five students stayed behind to give us their contact information.

After everyone finally dispersed, we walked slowly back to where we'd left the bikes, Elder Myre's pants still soggy. "Don't tell the others," he asked softly as we unchained our rides home.

"Elder Myre, this is a faith-promoting story. We have to tell *everyone*."

He didn't say anything. But I could see myself recounting the story in Institute classes, trying to encourage young men who hadn't yet gone on missions that that was where the Lord wanted them.

I was going to be good at retention.

But given that we had five potential new converts, perhaps I'd be good at baptizing, too. When you made good use of one talent, the Lord often gave you another. Wasn't there a parable somewhere about that?

We rode home in silence but then had a roaring good time sharing the news of our five contacts with the others. At least I did. We all had some cookies and milk, and then I put on my pajamas and climbed in bed, dreaming happily most of the night about vaginas, my mother's bosoms, and my girlfriend Cheryl's innocent smile.

# Till Death Do Us Part

"Michael died," said my husband Daniel as I walked through the door.

"Who's Michael?" I asked.

"Michael Monson."

"Oh, my God. What happened?"

"He killed himself, Billy."

I sat on the sofa in stunned silence. Michael and I had never been close. I'd picked him up in front of a Bartell's drugstore on Capitol Hill, and rather than take me to his place for sex, he brought me to an end-of-summer party in Rainier Beach in south Seattle. But at the party, I'd met Daniel. That was seven years ago. Daniel and I had been together ever since.

It had to have been a double blow for Michael, who'd earlier been set up on a date with Daniel by the hosts of that party. That date hadn't gone well, either. Still, as I'd only devoted half an hour to my relationship with Michael, I didn't feel like a lover of three years jilting him in public. It probably wasn't nice of me, but what are you going to do when you finally do meet the man of your dreams? Daniel was attractive, several years older than me at fifty-four, and a self-employed carpenter who set his own hours.

He was also a former Mormon, as I was. Beyond that, he had served in the same mission I had, Rome. And he'd even taught the sweet young woman who later became my fiancée for three years before I finally had the sense to come out. Paola had died last month of breast cancer, having never married. Her sister emailed me.

That news had come just days after Ari emailed me with the news that he had only months to live. Ari and I had dated briefly in New Orleans, and I'd quickly fallen head over heels for him, even considering converting to Judaism. Then one day he told me we couldn't date anymore, that he was marrying a guy from Lake Charles. As much as I loved Daniel, in some ways, I still thought of Ari as the man who got away.

His prostate cancer had now spread to his spine and his brain.

I hoped his partner would be okay.

I hadn't dated at all my first two years in Seattle, so Daniel and I went out for an agonizingly long six weeks before we had sex, at which time I learned that Daniel was exclusively a bottom. I was versatile, so I adapted to being exclusively a top relatively well. About a year and a half later, I moved into his home in Rainier Beach, selling the land my grandmother had left me in Mississippi when she'd died a few years earlier, and paying $90,000 toward the house. It was "our" house now.

Michael and I never hung out again.

Since moving to Seattle from New Orleans after Hurricane Katrina, I had never been able to make friends here. People were polite but not really friendly. One trick back on Capitol Hill had become a minor friend who I saw a couple of times a year. But as often as not, he'd plan a time for us to get together and then cancel at the last minute. So I didn't rely on his friendship very much.

Other than that, there was just Daniel. And he and I were in fact great friends. We had School Night on Mondays, listening to a college lecture on DVD. We had Italian Night on Tuesdays, when we only spoke Italian to each other. He saw longtime friends on Wednesday while I relaxed at home alone. Then on Thursday, we had Game Night, when we played Backgammon or Scrabble or chess. Friday night once a month was Book Club with some of his other friends. And Saturday night was Date Night, when we prepared a special meal and watched a DVD from Netflix. Sunday night was usually just a night to relax and watch PBS. That was also the night Daniel attended his AA meetings. He never divulged anything that took place there, but he was always noticeably more talkative when he returned home, so even though he didn't get back until 9:45, I always made sure to stay up so we could talk for another forty-five minutes or so.

"How did you find out?" I asked Daniel.

"Jerry told me." Jerry was one of the hosts of the party where we'd met. He was also part of the Book Club group. "Apparently, Michael had been ill lately, and he was depressed."

I could certainly understand that. When I'd been diagnosed with HIV sixteen years earlier, I'd fallen into a deep depression, too. I went from my usual 150 pounds down to 133 because I simply couldn't force myself to eat. I'd been on Prozac and Wellbutrin for a year and a half, but in some ways, I still hadn't fully recovered, even after all this time. I used to be very active, but with the depression, I began sleeping almost continually, and even now, on weekends I took several naps, and on weeknights, I was often in bed by 9:00. Of course, my crappy job had me borderline depressed anyway, so that didn't help. I hadn't been suicidal in a long while, though I did often hope to die in my sleep.

"You going to be okay?" asked Daniel.

"Me? Oh, sure," I replied.

"Depression and suicide are contagious."

"Well, how do *you* feel?" I countered. Daniel had been on anti-depressants ever since we'd met. His father had committed suicide ten years ago. Daniel had stopped his meds a couple of months back, though he admitted he still wasn't feeling great. While we talked about a lot of things, he rarely spoke to me about his depression and always put on a happy face, despite what he might really be feeling, afraid he'd depress *me* if he spoke about it. I was left most of the time in the dark, just hoping for the best.

"I'm good. I have Spanish class at the Hall tonight. You okay eating alone?"

"Sure, sure." About a year ago, Daniel had joined the Freedom Socialist Party here in Seattle. He now often missed School Night with me because he had School Night with them. On Monday nights, they'd get together to discuss some book about the history of socialism. On Italian Night, he went to the Hall to study Spanish with his friends there.

Daniel had *lots* of friends. He had quite a few from his twenty years in AA. He had his Book Club friends. Even after seven years, they were clearly his friends, not ours. He had his political friends. It felt so strange to have virtually no friends of my own when he had literally dozens and dozens. He was always off fixing a friend's fence or their faucet or helping someone move or jump their battery or whatever. On Saturdays, he even spent a couple of hours with a mentally ill man from AA, just helping him one-on-one with his steps, though he wasn't even the guy's sponsor.

Daniel was a great guy, there was no doubt about that.

"Okay, hon, I'll see you later. Gotta run." We kissed, and Daniel headed out the door.

I went in my office, took off my work shirt and put on a T-shirt, and took off my work pants. Daniel didn't like that I walked around the house in my boxer briefs, but it was in the 80's every afternoon and evening, and with no air conditioner, I simply didn't feel like wearing pants. I'd outgrown my shorts. In fact, I was up to 215 pounds now. I'd been 165 when I met Daniel. He was still at 175 where he'd been then, but I'd ballooned. Daniel never made an issue of it, sweetie that he was, but I shuddered when I looked in a mirror.

I opened a prepackaged salad from Safeway into a mixing bowl and sat down on the sofa. Since I'd been diagnosed with diabetes two weeks earlier, I was eating better. Whole grain bread instead of white. Turkey and chicken instead of red meat. Almonds and peanuts instead of chips. I'd lost a whopping one pound so far. Still, I felt better, and I was only urinating twelve times a day instead of eighteen. If I kept at it, and the metformin was effective, I might actually get better.

I watched MSNBC as I ate, but while Chris and Rachel and Lawrence were all great shows, I could only take so much reality at a time. Daniel could watch all three hours in a row, but I rarely watched more than fifteen minutes, going into my office to read *Calvin and Hobbes* or *The Far Side.* If I was feeling particularly energetic, I'd read a Mormon novel like *The*

*Moroni Deception* or *Destroying Angel.* I enjoyed keeping in touch with my culture.

In fact, if Daniel weren't so adamantly against the Church, I'd probably attend services once in a while. The Skyway ward was only a six-minute bus ride away. I'd tried going to movies with the Seattle Movie Bears downtown, but that was a one-hour trip both ways, and the guys simply watched the movie and then went home. There was no actual socializing. It seemed a lot of effort for so little reward. I'd also gone to La Tavola Italiana a few times. They met on Pioneer Square, but the folks who attended spoke so little Italian that I found the meetings frustrating.

I guess I didn't have friends because I didn't try hard enough.

Making friends at church had always been so easy, I thought regretfully. Of course, the church was not a social club. The leaders consistently made that very clear. But the truth was that while in the church, I'd always had plenty of friends. Getting excommunicated had been hard not only for the betrayal I felt from the leaders but also because my entire circle of friends disappeared overnight. But New Orleans was a friendly city, and the gay community there was no exception. I joined the Gay Men's Chorus and started going to the bars, and soon I had a whole new circle of friends.

That just hadn't worked here. Now I was older and fatter and not very popular at the bars. The Seattle Men's Chorus cost too much money to fully participate. While Daniel had a work truck, I was on public transportation, and it simply took too long to get anywhere in the city from way down in Rainier Beach. Daniel and I were both pleasant to the neighbors when we saw them, but they weren't interested in anything more than hi.

But at least I had Daniel. We watched *Roman Holiday* and *To Have and Have Not* and *Key Largo* and *North by Northwest*. We grew green beans and tomatoes and peppers together. He read articles from *Harper's* to me on the sofa. If it weren't for my crappy job, I'd be pretty happy, even with just the one friend, when the one friend was such a good one.

After I finished eating, I washed the dishes. Daniel always left several in the sink since he hated washing them. Then I went in my office and read some of *Latter-Day Cipher*. That kept me going until about 9:00. By then, I would normally have gone to bed, but I wanted to wait up for Daniel tonight. In fact, I thought I'd give him a surprise. We usually only had sex on Date Night, but we'd both just been getting over colds last Saturday and had skipped the sex. So tonight, I pulled out his dildo and his tit clamps and had them lying on the bed waiting for him.

But I did lie down to rest, keeping the light on so I'd be ready to jump out of bed when I heard his key in the lock.

Only I didn't hear his key in the lock. 9:30 passed, and then 10:00. When 10:30 came and went, I began to get worried. What if Daniel had a heart attack? He was in reasonably good shape, but he did smoke, and he was sixty-one now. Anything could happen. What if he'd been in a car accident? Rainier Avenue was hard to navigate in the best of circumstances. He could have hit a bus head on. He already had a crumpled front bumper from two other accidents he'd been in.

What if he'd deliberately run into a pole?

Oh, why did he have to leave his cell phone at home when he went to these meetings? He was addicted to that phone and the only way he could make himself avoid checking texts or calls was to leave it at home. So now I couldn't even call to see if he was all right.

I knew I was probably overreacting because of all the other bad news lately. Daniel probably just had a flat tire or something. His truck was way old and beat up.

But what if?

I did have three friends in New Orleans who'd been murdered over the years. Of course, Seattle had far less crime.

My last partner in New Orleans had died of liver cancer only days before the storm. I had a friend who'd died of emphysema. Several who'd died of AIDS. People did die.

What if Daniel had had a stroke? His mother had died of one, though she was eighty-seven when it happened.

What if some shooter had gone to the Hall and shot everyone to make a political point? Shooters showed up everywhere these days.

I bit my lip, trying to stop being ridiculous.

Daniel had run out of gas a couple of months ago. That's probably all it was now. He always waited too long to fill up.

I wondered if I would be this freaked out if Daniel wasn't the only person outside of work who ever talked to me.

Well, of course I would. He was my husband.

What was I going to do if Daniel died and left me all alone? My first thought was that I'd go back to church after all. But I'd read Thomas Wolfe's *You Can't Go Home Again* in college, and I knew he was right. At this point, church would seem familiar and yet altogether alien to me at the same time. And how could I ever comfortably socialize with people whose agenda was to eliminate me, no matter how "nice" they seemed? I wanted to believe I could go back, I longed to go back and feel the camaraderie I'd felt before, but I knew it couldn't happen. Once you no longer believed, what kind of glue was really there? I felt stupid and traitorous for even considering the possibility.

It was just that I wanted friends so badly.

I even tried hooking up with the ex-Mormon group here in Seattle. Only it turned out that every social they'd had since I joined took place in Kenmore or Issaquah or Tacoma or some other outlying town too difficult to get to by public transportation.

I remembered years ago visiting my friends Barbara and Keith. I had dated their daughter before my mission, and she'd married someone else while I was in Italy. It had been a relief to me, but they were sure I was devastated, and they insisted on being my friends when I returned home. I went to see them once a month in nearby Slidell and spent the day with them. We'd go swimming or play UNO or sit and talk about the Millennium. I was always impressed with how close they were but also concerned that while they considered each other their best friend, they really had no other friends. When Barbara eventually died from complications from her own diabetes, Keith was left with no one. He'd lived another twenty years, lonely that entire time. I did continue to write to him after I moved to Seattle, but we'd never been very close after I left the Church, and one day about a year ago, he stopped writing. I looked online and found an obituary.

I had to do something to make more friends.

Given my health, Daniel was much more likely to outlive me, even though I was only fifty-three, but he'd have friends and support, so he'd be just fine. It was me who was going to suffer if I was left alone.

Would God let him visit me once a week as a spirit, as an angel, as a ghost? I could get by if I could just see him once a week.

Of course, that was ridiculous. If he was gone, he was gone, and my life would never be the same.

It wasn't fair. We'd only been officially married just one year.

As much as I loved Daniel, I could see the danger of putting "all my eggs in one basket." Something had to change. But even if I did have other friends, I still never wanted to lose Daniel.

Where *was* he?

If he were in fact dead, and I was now all alone in the world, would I eventually end up suicidal again?

Soon it was 11:00, and I was pacing back and forth frantically. I called Harborview Medical Center, but they hadn't admitted Daniel. I called Swedish, but they hadn't heard of Daniel either. I was just on the verge of praying when I heard steps on the front porch. I ran to the door and opened it.

"What are you doing up? It's way past your bedtime."

"What happened?"

"Oh, I got a call from Howard this afternoon. I forgot to tell you." Howard was the mentally ill guy Daniel saw on Saturdays. "He was having a crisis, so I went over and talked to him for a while."

I hugged him.

"What's that all about?" He laughed.

"I love you."

"I love you, too."

As a Mormon, I'd always expected my marriage to last for eternity. As an ex-Mormon agnostic, I didn't know what to expect in the slightest. I just knew I'd better make the most of what I had now.

"Come in the bedroom," I said, motioning with my arm. "We're going to make up for Saturday night."

"Aren't you going to have a hard time getting up in the morning?"

"There are worse problems."

"How's your blood sugar?"

"Fine."

I pulled Daniel onto the bed and started unbuttoning his shirt, kissing him deeply as I tugged it off his body.

"Please, God, be real," I prayed silently. "And let Daniel and me be together forever, even without the temple."

I had this one good friend, and I was going to be the best friend to him that I could be. Maybe I'd have to become a Socialist, too, in order to spend more time with him. Or watch the full line-up on MSNBC. Or learn some basic carpentry. There were certainly more difficult sacrifices. But I wasn't going to miss out on the one friend I did have.

I picked up the dildo and smiled.

# An Endowed Spy

Jerrod stood at the newsstand and watched the woman walk by. In her mid-thirties, she was wearing a mottled gray suit coat over a scarlet red skirt, and sporting two-inch heels on narrow-toed red leather shoes. Her shoulder-length hair was almost black, every strand in place. If Jerrod had been a worldly man instead of a faithful Mormon, he might have been attracted to her.

No matter. Silicon had been clear. Jerrod was to approach the woman in a bar, seduce her, and then murder her once he was in her apartment.

Not murder. Assassinate. Why did Jerrod keep forgetting the distinction? He'd killed eleven people in the past year since being recruited by the Company after graduating from Brigham Young University with a degree in History, specifically, Mormon history. Why government agents in the Company felt his studies provided a useful background, Jerrod had never figured out. He had always expected to teach college Institute classes. His recruiter had insisted his selection was more due to his missionary service in Austria, but Jerrod had only been assigned to murder one Austrian so far.

Assassinate.

The woman was walking quickly up the street, and Jerrod followed briskly but carefully. He'd been observing her the past several evenings, and she had yet to go into a bar at all. But tonight was Friday, and the woman had walked right past her apartment building after getting off the subway. Perhaps tonight she needed a drink.

It had been awkward for Jerrod to take his first drink as part of the job. It had also been awkward the first time he'd had to use sex as a tool. But if killing for his country wasn't a sin, then why should lesser commandments be a problem? Every Sunday, Jerrod went to whichever LDS meetinghouse was nearby and made sure to partake of the sacrament. Then his soul was pure for another week.

The woman pushed open the glass door to a posh bar with a fancy neon sign proclaiming the place a "Delicate Edge." It had certainly been better than the grubby bar called "Rear Entrance" he'd had to frequent for three nights before murdering a dangerous gay hacker last month. He wished he hadn't had to go through with the sex that time before getting down to the killing. But he was nothing if not a gentleman.

Jerrod decided to wait on the sidewalk for another five minutes to make sure the woman wasn't coming right back out.

Silicon had been gruff with Jerrod when giving him the assignment. "No more of that ritualistic crap," she'd said. "Just strangle her with a scarf."

Jerrod had nodded his acceptance of the order, but he knew he could never comply. If a person had committed terrible sins, and Jerrod knew no one would be on the elimination list if they hadn't, then they needed more than just to die. Dying only helped the country. It didn't help the person being murdered.

Assassinated.

If Jerrod had learned anything at all during his four years studying at Brigham Young, it was that Blood Atonement was absolutely necessary for people to be forgiven of certain grievous sins. Otherwise they'd end up in Outer Darkness. Poison wasn't an option. With poison, the person didn't bleed. Strangling wasn't an option, either. Even if there were bruising from the choking, the key feature of Blood Atonement was that the blood be physically shed. The Church had actually practiced the principle back in the day. Maybe they still did secretly. Gentiles simply didn't understand. It was why Utah continued to have a firing squad for so many years rather than institute hanging or the electric chair. So when Jerrod was assassinating someone, radiation poisoning was out. So was a blow to the head. Even a gunshot to the head wouldn't work, in Jerrod's opinion. It was essential that the person *be aware* that they were bleeding, be aware that they were shedding their blood for their sins. Jerrod always made sure to explain it to his victims.

Assignments.

Of course, it was Christ's atonement that did the bulk of the work of forgiveness. It was simply that some particularly bad sins had to be helped along by the blood of the sinner. Brigham Young had made it quite clear. And there was no reason Jerrod couldn't serve his country *and* save souls at the same time, was there?

Five minutes had passed, so Jerrod casually entered the building and walked up to the bar without looking about. After ordering a scotch, he leaned against the counter and slowly surveyed his surroundings. The woman was seated at a table about three yards away, sitting alone, sipping from a glass filled with a dark liquid. Her eyes were closed, and she leaned her head back, sighing.

Jerrod would disembowel her later. All eleven of his assignments had been killed either by having their throats slit or by being disemboweled. That's the way Mormons were threatened with death in the temple if they ever revealed any secrets, so Jerrod knew that was the way Heavenly Father wanted his non-Mormon children murdered, too.

Silicon had grown increasingly irritated with Jerrod, however. While killing a woman in this way could sometimes be disguised as a sex crime, it was difficult to disembowel a high-ranking male military official without it looking suspicious. Jerrod had to prove himself tonight. He had to make things right with the Company.

Could he simply stab the woman in the chest?

Doing such a thing just felt wrong. Jerrod had more than once wondered if he would one day need to atone for his sins himself by shedding his own blood. But that would be like asking every soldier who ever fought in a war to be killed merely for protecting his homeland. Some killings weren't sins. Even Nephi was ordered to kill an unarmed man.

But would there be time for the woman to understand why she was bleeding before she lost consciousness? It was essential that she understand. Jerrod didn't want to be cruel, after all.

The woman looked toward the bar. Jerrod continued to look in her direction until their eyes made contact. After a brief moment, he turned and looked in another direction. You couldn't seduce someone if you looked too anxious.

Jerrod thought about the endowment session he'd attended the afternoon before. If possible, he enjoyed going to the temple on his assignments in exotic cities. He'd joked to Silicon once that he might one day write a story called "Murderer with a Recommend." She hadn't looked amused.

Naturally, Jerrod could tell no one about his work. The job made marriage an absolute impossibility. That had worried him for a while, since temple marriage was essential for attaining the Celestial Kingdom. But he was only twenty-seven, and by the look on Silicon's face when she gave him this assignment, it might well be his last. He'd disembowel the woman, get fired, and apply with the Church Educational System after all. Tonight would make a dozen murders. Twelve was a righteous number. He could retire after twelve.

Jerrod glanced back toward the woman. She was looking out the window, but a moment later, she turned and looked toward the bar again. Their eyes met and lingered a bit longer this time before Jerrod turned away.

Still, he didn't really *want* to retire. He liked his job. He'd never felt so important in his entire life. He was *doing* things.

Maybe he would in fact just go ahead and stab the woman in the chest as he'd considered earlier. That would satisfy Silicon. Then he could stay with the Company. He could always get married when he was the woman's age. There'd still be plenty of time to raise kids in the gospel.

Taking another sip of his scotch, Jerrod turned casually back toward the woman. He stiffened when he realized she was gone. Had she taken off for the bathroom? Had she left the building? Damn!

He just barely caught sight of a red skirt and mottled gray jacket through the front window and jumped up from his stool. He hurried out of the bar and started trying to close the gap between himself and the woman. Half a block behind her, he wondered if he'd have to wait for another evening. It wouldn't be the end of the world. The woman might go out again on Saturday night. It wasn't as if these things had to be done immediately.

Still, it would be nice to be finished and be able to wipe the slate clean again on Sunday morning with a thimbleful of water and a pinched piece of white Wonder bread.

He picked up his pace.

The woman paused to give money to a beggar, and this made Jerrod pause as well. What kind of deadly enemy gave money to beggars? He realized he rarely knew what any of his assignments were actually guilty of. He was told to take care of them, and that's what he did. It wasn't so very different from obeying his mission president. Or his bishop. Or the prophet.

He'd almost caught up with the woman by the time she started walking again. "That was nice of you," he said, hoping he was close enough that she could hear.

The woman turned in confusion as if hearing a buzzing noise, and then her eyes focused on him. "For those to whom much is given, much is required," she said with a smile.

Jerrod tried not to look surprised. "How much did you give him?" he asked. He didn't know why he asked such a question.

"Five dollars. No point giving anything less with the cost of food these days." She shrugged.

"Or the cost of a bottle."

She shrugged again. "Not my place to judge."

Jerrod had become good at small talk but found himself now at a loss for words. Still, he'd made contact. If the woman went back to the bar tomorrow night, he'd have a better chance at connecting then.

"Do you judge people?" the woman asked with a sly smile.

No, Jerrod thought. Someone else does. I'm just the guy who enforces the sentence. "Only if they have particularly sordid sex," he replied. He had to try to be flirtatious.

The woman laughed, a lovely, tinkling sound. "And what qualifies as sordid?" she asked, again smiling as if she had a secret.

"That depends on what we can negotiate," said Jerrod, also smiling. The woman looked even more attractive than she had earlier. He felt a stirring in his groin.

"Your suit is very nice," said the woman. "Armani?"

Jerrod smiled in response. It wasn't Armani, but he would go along.

"And a hundred dollar tie?"

"A hundred and fifty."

"How often do *you* give to the poor?" she asked, still smiling.

Jerrod paid his tithing. And put aside a little each month for a down payment on a house. There wasn't enough left over for much else. "Would you like to take a walk and give out five dollar bills tonight?" he asked. He was just trying to catch the woman's interest in some way, but the idea actually intrigued him. Why *didn't* he do things like that?

What could this woman possibly be guilty of?

"Maybe later," she said. "Why don't you come up to my place for a drink first?"

Jerrod smiled. The woman turned and nodded for him to follow. They were only a few yards from the door to her building, and soon they were in the elevator going up to the fifteenth floor. Her apartment was sleek and modern, clean, with only a single book, closed, on the coffee table. The woman took off her jacket and laid it across the top of a high-backed chair.

"Scotch?" she asked.

Jerrod's eyebrows arched. Had she been watching him at the bar from the beginning? Or was it a lucky guess?

"Sure," he said.

"I'm a rum and Coke girl myself," she said. She went to a small bar and prepared the drinks.

She handed him a glass and he took a sip. The woman took a deep sip of hers and leaned her head back and sighed as she'd done in the bar. She had a lovely throat.

Jerrod wanted to slit it.

Still, the woman seemed decent enough. Was it possible he was killing people who didn't deserve to die? He knew it was bad to follow a leader blindly like a mindless sheep, and yet, didn't Jesus always talk about his sheep in a fond, positive way? The scriptures said that obedience was the most important thing.

Maybe he should just leave the apartment. Tell Silicon he quit right now. He'd done enough for his country. Someone else could take over for a while. Even God didn't expect a missionary to serve forever.

If he had sex with the woman, without the intent to kill her, would that be a sin?

Jerrod looked at the woman, sitting on the sofa with her legs crossed, and wanted nothing more in the world than to marry her.

How ridiculous.

He put his hand on his suit pocket and felt for the knife he had there.

"You know," said the woman, looking at him with a coy expression, "I always like to tell my assignments why I'm killing them."

Jerrod gasped involuntarily, just at the same moment he felt his heart burning as if it were on fire. He put his hand on his chest and staggered to the chair where the woman's coat had been placed so carefully.

"When we have dupes killing allies of the U.S., we always figure they'll catch on sooner or later that they've been playing for the wrong team. One year is the most we ever give anyone."

Jerrod could hardly hear the last words, the blood was drumming in his ears so loudly. It felt as if that man from Rear Entrance was sitting on his chest again.

Why couldn't the woman have been decent enough to have sex with him before she killed him? Jerrod was always considerate enough to have sex first. He was reasonably well-endowed. It was the least he could do for his victims.

Assignments.

No. Victims.

Jerrod fumbled with his suit jacket, trying desperately to pull out the knife and slice his own throat before he stopped breathing, but his hands wouldn't work. He fell onto the floor and looked up into the woman's beautiful face.

"This isn't even my apartment," she said, still sitting calmly.

Jerrod thought of missionary devotionals, and Seminary classes, and BYU student wards, and the pretty young girls he'd passed up for his job. He thought about Celestial rooms and General Conference and Fast and Testimony offerings.

He was a good man.

His last thought was whether or not there would be Institute classes to teach in hell.

# The Girl Next Store

Retirement is *fabulous*. I'm 65 and quit my job three months ago, and I've never been happier. I sleep late when I want to. I stay up late when I want to. I go to movies in the middle of the day. I wear comfortable clothes and comfortable shoes. I don't have to put on make-up anymore. I take naps. I leave my condo on Lake Washington and drive out to Snoqualmie Falls or Leavenworth or whatever other place catches my fancy.

I can just be myself, something I haven't been able to do in many, many years.

The problem is: what if your natural self isn't all sweetness and pie?

Last week at the bus stop, an old Chinese man came up to me and rubbed my belly as if I were the Buddha. It wasn't a sexual touch. He was clearly just making fun of me because of my pot belly. I'm 5'4" and weigh about 195 pounds. I'm trying to keep it under 200, believe me. But I've never had the best eating habits, and it all shows up in my stomach. At Book Club, the other members have no qualms about patting me on my belly as they walk by, or making comments if I drop food while I'm eating.

You know, you drop just as much food when you're thin. It's just that you don't have a huge drop cloth of a body to catch everything like when you're fat.

I've always found the fact that people feel free to condescend and tell me how to live my life tiresome, yet I've dealt with it for the most part. My boss used to tell me, "Put on a white beard and you could play Santa Claus" and then laugh as if that were funny.

I don't have to see *him* anymore.

Retirement is fabulous.

But the other day as I was walking down the street, a twenty-something with a smart-alecky attitude pointed at me and said, "So when are you due?"

That's when it happened. That's when I knew I had to rethink my plans for the afterlife. That's when I knew I had to "be myself."

The young man lived in my neighborhood, so I casually walked behind him at a good distance so he didn't know I was following him. I found where he lived, and after another couple of stakeouts, I discovered which car was his. I returned another night with my X-Acto knife and slit his tires. Or tried to. It's not easy these days since they make tires so much stronger now. I ended up just scratching the paint on his car instead.

Was that mean of me?

Well, who the fuck cares?

I didn't tell my bishop, but I did skip partaking of the sacrament the following Sunday. And I thought and prayed and fasted (a little) as I tried to decide what to do next.

Back before I joined the LDS Church, I'd lived what must have been considered at the time "a wild life." When I was eighteen and still blond, I dated a 28-year-old black man who played in a band with Jimmy Hendrix. Tyrone slept with a lot of women but tried to make me feel special, at least at first, by writing me a card that said I wasn't like all the others, that I was the perfect "girl next store."

It was only after he hit me that I started making fun of his poor English. Of course, that didn't help matters. We broke up after only four months.

My parents were relieved, I can tell you that.

When I left Tyrone, I slit his tires. That was easier to do back then. Not deeply enough for them to go flat, but just enough that they might blow out while he was driving down the freeway at 60 miles an hour.

Unfortunately, his tires did go flat.

I was just being myself.

People talk all the time as if being oneself is a good thing, the ultimate act of self-love one can experience.

A few months after my time with Tyrone, I met a beautiful Japanese girl, and we became lovers. My parents were horrified all over again. We were together for six months, until Sue admitted to me that she'd poisoned my Yorkie because it peed on her slippers. I slit her tires too and moved back in with my parents.

And that's when my life changed. Two Mormon missionaries stopped by, and my parents let them in. I listened with indifference at first, but soon their ideas began to intrigue me. I had already seen that being myself meant being a vengeful libertine. Perhaps there really was a better way. Three weeks later, I was baptized.

Now, as a "respectable" young woman, I went to college and soon began working for King County. While I still liked men as well as women, I liked women more and so stopped dating altogether. At church, I could never hold a really high position because I'd never married, but I taught Sunday school and Primary and the Beehives. In my personal life, I took in a homeless woman for six months. I took in my brother's eighteen-year-old daughter for a year, when they weren't getting along, even letting her take over my bedroom while I slept on the sofa. The Church taught me to be loving and caring and giving, and that's the way I lived my life.

I enjoyed it well enough, but deep down, I kept thinking, "I can't wait to retire." And I meant it not only in regard to my job at the county, but also in regard to my life at church. It was stifling in some low level way that chafed but was still just minimally bearable. I *wanted* to fuck that pretty woman in Accounting. I *wanted* to drink tequila. I *wanted* to slit my neighbor's tires when he let his dog poop in front of my building every day and never picked it up.

But I had to live my life so that up in Heaven, some old white guy with a little dick and five other wives would add me to his harem.

Greek gods didn't have to be nice. Why did Mormon gods? Why couldn't I just be myself?

This week, I was taking a long walk to get some exercise. I'd lost two pounds since retiring. Sometimes, I drove to Seward Park and walked, and sometimes, I just walked in my neighborhood. Today I was walking along Lake Washington, surely one of the most beautiful paths in Seattle. I was enjoying the breeze, watching the sailboats out on the lake, and smiling pleasantly at the joggers and bike riders I passed along the way.

It's not as if I were a jerk.

But one woman was running with her unleashed dog, which I assume must normally have been well-behaved. It was mid-sized, though I couldn't tell the breed. As they passed me, I raised my hand to wave, and the dog actually nipped me. I pulled my hand back in surprise, seeing just a drop of blood, and the woman shouted, "Leave my dog alone!"

These little unpleasantries happen every day. You learn to just take them in stride. It's not like this was the first time I'd ever been bitten. But today, I thought of the Roman gods. They didn't have to be nice. I picked up a rock and threw it at the woman. It hit her in the head. She yelled and ran faster.

When I returned home, I wrote a small check and mailed it to the Fistula Foundation.

It's not as if I were an asshole.

Things continued much like this for the next few weeks. Then today at church, Sister Hawking, who reminded me of a grown up Nellie Olson, came over to me in Relief Society and said sweetly, "Oh, I just love the way you can wear the same dress over and over and over and always make it look new by wearing a different scarf." I was wearing my favorite purple dress with yellow daisies. It always made me feel good. Sister Hawking smiled and inspected the scarf more closely. "Oh, wait, that's the same scarf, too, isn't it?" She chuckled and shook her head. "Silly me."

I smiled just as sweetly in return and replied, "You're not silly" as I waved dismissively at the air in her direction. "You're a vicious old bat who thinks she's better than everyone else because she married for money rather than for love. I guess that makes you a prostitute." I was still smiling kindly as I finished.

Norse gods didn't have to be nice.

I was called in to the bishop's office when our meetings ended that day, and the bishop asked me if anything was wrong. "I'm retired," I said. "That means I'm getting old. I can't help but start seriously thinking about the afterlife."

"Yes?" the bishop replied slowly.

"I know we spend our whole lives preparing for Judgment Day and trying to make it to the Celestial Kingdom so we can become gods."

"Uh-huh?" he said, a little uncertain.

"It's only that now it feels more real. I'll actually be on the other side in a few years. If my doctor is right about my cholesterol, it could be any day."

The bishop looked confused. "Then why have you been acting so nasty the past few weeks?" he asked. "Several of the other women have mentioned it to me."

"Have you ever read the Old Testament?" I asked.

The bishop looked a little uncomfortable. "Well, not the *entire* book," he admitted.

I nodded. "Have you read enough to notice that the god of the Old Testament isn't very nice?"

The bishop shook his head in protest. "God is stern but loving. Always."

"You should perhaps finish reading the book," I said. "The guy's a jerk."

The bishop gasped. "Sister Gray, don't say such things!"

"Bishop, I'm perfectly fine with this realization. In fact, it's quite a relief."

The bishop still looked confused. "I don't understand."

I shrugged. "Hindu gods don't have to be nice."

"That's because they're not real," said the bishop, shaking his head. "Real gods have to be perfect. You have to start behaving yourself again."

"Bishop," I said slowly, "this week I spoke to a woman in the park about my age. She was very nice, talked about her cats."

"Yes?" He looked lost again. He was clearly not enjoying the conversation.

"So I went home with her, we had some tea, and then I went down on her. It was so wonderful just to be myself again after all this time."

The bishop's mouth fell open.

"I had sex with a black lady the next day. And a Chinese woman the day after that. Being retired is fabulous. I feel like a kid again."

"Sister Gray," said the bishop, his voice trembling, "I think you may have had a stroke. We have to get you evaluated."

"I just wonder how you can ever achieve greatness, or godhood, for that matter, if you're spending your whole life being someone besides yourself."

The bishop looked at me a long moment. "We're going to have to hold a court on you."

"A court of love?" I asked with a smile. "You guys can be just as mean as God."

The bishop's mouth fell open again.

I stood up and headed for the door, but just before I left, I turned around and faced the bishop again. I reached into my purse and pulled out my X-Acto knife. "I'm a Mormon," I said. "And one day I'll be a Mormon god. I finally realized Mormon gods don't have to be nice, either. Look at Brigham Young. He was no angel. And now he's on his way to becoming a god." I paused and smiled sweetly, the way I had with Sister Hawking, and twisted the blade to let it reflect in the light. "So I'd think twice about excommunicating me."

I left the bishop alone with his thoughts and walked slowly out of the building and to my car. I drove with the windows down, enjoying the breeze in my hair. I pulled into one of those new marijuana stores that had opened in the past year and parked. Happily fingering my favorite Sunday dress, I bought some pot. I lit it in the car and drove home along the lake, singing an old Jimmy Hendrix song and thinking about big black dicks.

# Star Fleet Testing

I was mostly a lurker. Like an extra in the background from a scene set in Ten Forward, with Whoopi at the bar. An inappropriate comparison, I suppose, considering I didn't drink. But sometimes I felt like a lurker at church, too, as fathers blessed their babies and saw their sons and daughters off on missions. I felt as if I spent most of my life watching and not doing. It had taken me years to even bother looking at Facebook, and once I began, I still didn't feel the need to interact very often. People put up photos of their dog, or their mother's hat, or the polishing they did of their bathroom doorknob. They went on at length about what they had for lunch, or the long line at the bank, or what they thought of their neighbor's new drapes.

No one ever messaged me personally. The only interaction was if they posted what was essentially an exceptionally brief diary entry and I felt the need to "like" it.

But millions and millions of people related to each other this way and seemed to enjoy it, so perhaps I was being too close-minded. My wife Nina and I ate dinner without the TV on, and even if we did watch a couple of shows every evening, we always set aside time to work together on a puzzle, or plan a party for some of our friends from church, or read to each other, or do anything that would allow us to interact as participants and not as spectators.

And still I felt like a lurker most of the time.

While Nina and I did not have any children ourselves, and probably never would, now that we were in our early forties, all of our friends at church in our Sacramento ward did. And they always reminded us how unfortunate we were to be childless. Said with kindness, of course. As well as an air of superiority.

Because we didn't always relate to hearing about problems surrounding kids, we didn't get invited over to other people's houses very often, despite our own parties. People would shake my hand at church and then seem to want nothing more to do with me. Unless it was time to ask for help on a service project. I would sit in the chapel every Sunday, watching Nina up on the stand directing music, and see all the smiling faces in the congregation, and feel utterly alone.

So I lurked. I suppose I was still hoping for a real connection somewhere. Nina and I helped raise funds for Elizabeth Warren. We helped collect money for the Red Cross. We helped give out food with Jewish Family Services. But while we might volunteer with other likeminded people, everyone usually just focused on doing their job, not on becoming friends. Nina didn't seem as bothered by it as I was. She'd just pick up a novel and read in bed. But I was back to Facebook. I'd dutifully go through everything posted, but try as I might, I consistently found it hard to reply to anything.

"My friend Abigail's home was destroyed in a tornado last night," posted one friend from my old Single Adult group from twenty years ago. "She broke her arm and lost everything she had." I was checking the latest comments submitted right before dinner. People seemed to post around the clock. The old Single Adult gang all still kept in touch, though we were now scattered across the country. All the others had children by now, though a couple of folks from the gang were single again.

"I'm so sorry for her loss," one person replied. "My prayers are with her."

"My condolences," wrote another.

"I send all my positive energy her way," said one more.

"All my love."

"I'll be praying for her."

"Sending my prayers to our wonderful Heavenly Father."

There were about fifteen responses in total, all much like these. Part of me wondered at the possibility of having so many friends, but something about the interaction still bothered me, though I couldn't quite put my finger on it. I neglected to add my name to the list and signed off instead.

That night, Nina sat next to me on the sofa while we watched *Person of Interest.* "Boy, my feet really hurt tonight," she said. "Standing in new shoes at work all day."

"Put your lovely feet in my lap," I returned. She did and I started rubbing them as we watched the show.

"I sure like this series," said Nina, twitching her toes in pleasure, whether at the massage or the TV screen, I couldn't tell.

"I find it kind of frustrating," I returned, nodding toward the set.

"Why is that?"

"On the one hand, I see the importance of trying to help just one person, but on the other, they're only getting numbers for one single person a week in New York, the largest city in America, and they *aren't* getting numbers for anyone anywhere else in the country, or the rest of the world, either, for that matter. It's like trying to save a beach from erosion, one grain of sand at a time."

"But it's interesting and exciting," she said.

"It *is* that," I agreed, fingering her toes. After a moment, I added, "And I suppose it teaches us the importance of taking a risk to help others."

"Not everything is a Sunday school lesson, Derek."

I laughed. "I think sometimes Heavenly Father does talk to us through TV shows," I protested. "When I was a kid, I used to watch this program called *Stingray*. It was about a man who spent all his time going around helping people in trouble. As he did it, he asked for favors from other people he'd helped out earlier, in a kind of pay-it-forward fashion. I used to think Nick Mancuso was one of the Three Nephites."

"It's possible you watch too much TV."

"Ninety minutes a night, just like you, even as a kid."

"Maybe it's time to work on another puzzle." Nina clicked the remote to turn off the television, smiling as she took my hand to lead me to the puzzle table we had set up near the window. "I bought a new one of the planet Earth from space. 1500 pieces."

"Too bad nobody else likes puzzles," I said, sitting down and opening the box. "My grandma told me when she was a teenager, she and all her friends would get together on Sunday to put a puzzle together. It was a communal activity. What do kids do these days?"

"We don't have to worry about what kids do these days." Nina started laying out all the pieces on the table.

"Shopping at the mall just doesn't sound as meaningful."

"What's meaningful is doing something together, whatever it is."

I nodded and started looking for border pieces. They were all the color of space.

The following day at work, my supervisor, Suzanne, who everybody loved, was quitting to start at a rival company for higher pay. While I would miss her, I was also worried about what jerk we might get in her place. Our department ordered two huge platters of Mexican food, but before we started eating, Suzanne gave a little speech, telling us all how much she'd miss us. Then she grabbed a huge cloth bag and began pulling items out. "For you, Jen, because you have a heart the size of Texas…" Suzanne gave her a large stuffed red heart. "For you, Margaret, because you always said you liked this scarf, it's yours now." She handed Margaret her favorite scarf. "Bill, because you're a miserable sexist and always called me a doll, I give you this." She handed him a Barbie doll, and everyone laughed, except Jen, the girl with the large heart, who glared at him. "Allen, because you're such a stuffed suit, I thought you could use these." She handed him a pair of brilliantly wild socks, half pink, half chartreuse, with lines and dots. He accepted them with an embarrassed smile. Suzanne continued with her gifts, joking, "I think I've learned more about giving from *The Wizard of Oz* than from my pastor." After addressing a few more coworkers, she finally turned to me. "Derek, because I hear you say such sweet and romantic things to your wife when you call to tell her you're on your way home, I give you this bottle of wine." I smiled as I picked it up, wondering if I should give it to our bishop at Tithing Settlement, as part of my income.

Back at my desk, I thought about the expense of all those gifts. It wasn't as if any of us were actually friends. Not really. Besides, if anything, we should all have been buying *her* gifts. Yet despite the inappropriateness of some of the presents, I could tell most of the staff felt touched by her efforts.

On Facebook that night, I saw a post by someone from my mission group. "My aunt's home was flooded by a freak storm. Just the bottom floor, but she lost all her best furniture. She's old and on Social Security and has homeowner's insurance but not flood."

The responses were similar to those of the other night. "I'm so sorry for her loss!"

"I wish her the best!"

"My prayers are with her."

"I'll send good thoughts her way."

"Isn't that your aunt who left the Church?"

"It's the Last Days, you know."

"I'll pray for her."

"Maybe this will bring her back. It's really a blessing."

"God works in mysterious ways."

I didn't post a response.

Friday evening, Nina and I went to our monthly Star Trek meeting, the highlight of the month.

I wondered why Fast and Testimony meeting wasn't the highlight of each month.

Nina and I often talked about how we would create stars and planets of our own one day, and how the Star Trek shows could give us some good ideas. As nerdy as some of the other attendees were, they could still be relatable in a way the Relief Society president wasn't. A few of the folks who came wore costumes, and sometimes a couple of people in the group would play three dimensional chess. We usually watched an episode, from any of several old series, that we'd voted for at the previous meeting. And sometimes we just played Star Trek trivia.

No one here minded that we didn't have kids.

As the meeting was drawing to an end, Samuel, a young man in his mid-twenties who always wore Vulcan ears, came up to me. "Derek, I'm going out of town next weekend. Would you be able to check in on my dog for a couple of days? He can get out in the back yard by himself through the doggie door, but he'll still want some attention and to go on a couple of walks."

"No problem, Sam."

"If you like," added Nina, "we could actually spend the weekend at your place and housesit, too. No charge."

"Really?"

"Sure. We like to have sex in other people's beds sometimes. So hard to do when you're both married and Mormon."

Samuel laughed.

The bishop's wife wouldn't have laughed.

"That bed's already seen lots of sleepovers," Samuel said with a smile. "A couple more bodies won't hurt. Just be sure to change the sheets before you leave."

"Not a problem. But if you have any Nutella around the house, for heaven's sake, hide it. Derek is a fiend."

"Nutella is an evil plot," I said, "sent from the future by the Terminators to destroy the human race."

"Wrong show," said Samuel.

Saturday after I weeded the garden for a while, I went with Nina to do the grocery shopping, and then we continued with our puzzle as we listened to the radio. A radical environmentalist was making fun of the NGOs that had lots of followers and raised lots of money for conservation but didn't do anything drastic enough to make a difference. "They got almost 400,000 people to march around Central Park," the man complained, "but that was just a photo op. They didn't even march by the United Nations building. It's all show but no substance. The next day, a mere thousand protestors marched on Wall Street, to protest where the real problem is."

The speaker irritated me. There'd been no accompanying rally or march here in Sacramento, which had been disappointing. I gave regularly to the Sierra Club and the Nature Conservancy, though I'd recently read that the Nature

Conservancy actually allowed oil drilling on some of their land, so maybe the guy had a point. I'd planted over six hundred trees with American Forests, though. I wondered how many trees the holier-than-thou protestor on the radio had planted. Or what he'd actually accomplished in changing how corporations polluted that the larger groups hadn't.

"Maybe next weekend when we dog-sit," suggested Nina, "we can go to the park, and while I tend to the dog, you can pull up some non-native species."

I inserted a piece of Africa into the puzzle.

"What difference can *I* make?" I asked. "The problems are too big. It will take massive government intervention to save this planet."

"Big government?" asked Nina, laughing. "Don't say that too loud, or we'll get called before a Church court."

I smiled. "I'm sure we're already on someone's list for being part of the Mormon Democrats Facebook group."

I inserted a piece of the Sahara desert.

"Doing the right thing doesn't always bring you friends." Nina held up a piece of the puzzle and wrinkled her nose as she considered where to put it.

I stopped and stared at her for a long moment.

Before getting ready for bed later, I checked my Facebook feed again. Another of my old Single Adult friends had posted. This was from Shelly, who still lived here in Sacramento in a neighboring ward. "Just finished my first round of chemo. Doctors don't know if it'll help or not. I'm sick as a dog."

There were the usual responses. "My prayers are with you."

"I'll put your name on the temple prayer roll."

"I'm sending all my positive energy your way."

"God never gives us more than we can handle."

"It's a test. The Lord only tests those he has faith in."

"Just remember that Heavenly Father loves you. We all love you."

"Keep going to church. You'll need the strength it gives you."

Sitting there reading that, the futility of life suddenly struck me. What could I do to really help Shelly? What could I do to fight political corruption? What could I do to save the environment? What could I do to cure Parkinson's? To end poverty? To stop war? Or human trafficking? Or child abuse? Or gang fighting? Or *anything*?

What could I do to develop enduring relationships, surely one of the most important tasks we faced on Earth?

I tried to think what my Church leaders would tell me, but as I looked at all these responses from other Mormons, I felt only disgust.

With friends like these…

Then a thought occurred to me from a recent Star Trek meeting. We'd watched a movie, *The Wrath of Khan*, and the idea of the Kobayashi Maru test had left a deep impression, though I'd seen the movie almost a dozen times before.

What if Earth life were *deliberately* a no-win situation? What if we *couldn't* solve any of the pressing problems of the world? What if it were *set up* that way on purpose? Perhaps it was all a character test, to see how we would react to serious, grave emergencies, *knowing* we were going to lose.

I sometimes dreamed of winning the lottery, though as a Mormon, I wasn't even allowed to buy a ticket. But I thought of all the good I could do with a hundred million dollars. In reality, of course, I could win a billion dollars and it would still be almost useless. A hundred billion dollars. Four trillion dollars. And I still wouldn't have enough money to solve the world's problems. So what good was my measly hundred million going to do?

Or the fifty dollars I actually had.

So many religious people felt that everything was in God's hands. They washed their own of the problem without a second thought. But Mr. Saavik didn't have the choice of passing off her Kobayashi Maru to a superior officer. It was *her* test. Passing the buck didn't show character.

I wondered why I didn't get lessons like this from the Book of Mormon.

So what was the answer to the Star Fleet test? Make a token effort? Do nothing at all?

Or do your very best, despite knowing the outcome?

Is that how one was eventually able to travel the star systems and inhabit other worlds?

I looked at Shelly's post online and decided not to lurk any longer. Do *something*, I told myself. Do anything. "I'll be at your home tomorrow morning at 10:00 to take care of your laundry and vacuuming." I hit enter, and then after thinking a moment, I added another line. "Oh, and my prayers are with you."

I logged out and then went downstairs to tell Nina why I'd be skipping church in the morning. We hadn't missed a meeting in years. We felt we had to be extra diligent to make up for our childlessness.

But Nina smiled and put her hand on mine. "I'll clean the bathrooms while you vacuum," she said.

Maybe one good relationship was enough to leave this world with.

It was 10:30, our usual bedtime, but Nina nodded toward the puzzle table. "We're almost done," she said. "Let's finish putting the Earth together before we go to bed."

I kissed her and we sat back down. I picked up a piece of the ocean and looked for the empty space where it belonged.

# My Path to the Gutter

I admit, I've always been rebellious. I used to sneak in a doughnut on Fast and Testimony Sundays. I used to pay tithing on my net and not my gross. I used to have an arrangement with three of my Visiting Teaching assignments that I would tell the Relief Society president I'd done my Visiting Teaching and they wouldn't tell anyone I hadn't. My worst act of rebellion was leaving BYU after one semester and transferring to the University of Utah.

There, I fell in with a rough crowd. One of my friends had a lip piercing. Another had blue hair. One girl wore sleeveless dresses. And another had a tattoo on her ankle.

My mother was quite worried.

The years passed, and I was flouting more of the commandments, twenty-seven and still unmarried, that rebellious streak still running strong. One day, my bishop called me into his office.

"Sister Campbell," he said warmly, "I see you haven't been paying your tithing the past couple of months. Is there a problem?"

"Heavenly Father is all powerful. I'm not. I don't understand why God needs my money when I'm barely getting by."

"Sister Campbell, the Lord has given you everything that you have. You're giving him just a token to show that you love him."

I frowned. "But when I give my friends and family gifts, I don't expect them to give me ten percent back because they love me."

"That's different."

"How so?"

Now the bishop frowned. "Let me read you a scripture."

"I have to leave now, Bishop." I stood up and started for the door.

"Sister Campbell, we still need to address your Visiting Teaching."

I opened the door and walked out. I heard the bishop saying, "You're heading down a slippery path, Sister," as I continued walking away.

Sundays were also my days to visit my family in Sandy, not a far drive even though I still lived up by the university. The afternoons were always grueling, and I'd begun missing once or twice a month, telling my mother I had to work. That simply gave her two reasons to be upset, but I was okay with that. I couldn't miss today, of course, because my youngest brother had just turned eight and had been baptized. The thought of having nine children over a span of twenty years as my mother had done sounded horrific, but since I had still not even begun my childbearing, I knew I wouldn't have to face the same fate.

Being a rebel had its advantages.

"Hey there, Robert," I said, shaking my brother's hand ceremoniously, "you're a big boy now. You've reached the Age of Accountability."

"Don't start," said my mother.

"I'm sure he's made a thorough study of Mormonism, Catholicism, Judaism, Islam, Buddhism, and all the other religions practiced in Salt Lake, and made his decision to join the Mormon Church after serious debate." I smiled at Robert. He looked at me blankly.

"Pauline..." said my mother warningly.

I turned to her. "Well, Mom, *you* believe he's reached an age where he can make momentous, life-altering decisions for himself, don't you?"

She looked at me suspiciously.

"Why don't you ask him to choose his own meals from now on?" I suggested. "And pick his own bedtime?"

Robert's eyes lit up.

"Pauline, he's an impressionable boy," said my mother. "I think we might have to ask you to stop coming over for Sunday dinner."

I smiled.

"And I'll start coming to your place alone instead."

I stopped smiling. The truth was that I didn't know why I said all these things to upset her. I knew a mature person would have a live and let live attitude. But I felt *compelled* to be a pain in the butt. It must be something like an addiction, I figured. Some people felt compelled to drink alcohol. I felt compelled to be contrary. I couldn't help myself.

But that didn't mean I didn't actually still believe. A little bit, anyway. When I'd pick up my Book of Mormon and then decide it was too boring to read, I felt Satan claiming just a little more of my soul. When I let the sacrament tray pass me by without partaking, I felt a little closer to Outer Darkness. When I refused to pay my fast offering, I felt more and more selfish every month.

I didn't just *feel* selfish, I realized. I *was* selfish.

It was just that I'd learned the money we gave to different Church programs didn't necessarily go to those programs. The Church donations slip had fine print at the bottom that explained the Church could use the funds provided any way they saw fit, despite the intent of the donor.

Things like that made me want to rebel.

To be honest, though, some of the Mormon doctrines still sounded appealing to me. For instance, the idea of eternal progression. I *liked* thinking my "intelligence," or my deepest essence, had always existed and would always continue to exist. As much as life sucked sometimes, I liked being able to think of it as a test. That seemed to explain the general discomfort well enough. And I definitely liked the idea of making very small, very tiny advances toward being a better person, and that God gave us literally millions of years to reach perfection. It didn't have to be done during this lifetime, or even in the next one or two hundred years. We could each advance at our own pace.

If there were any truth to the afterlife at all, this approach kind of made sense to me.

Of course, I wasn't about to tell my mother that.

We made it through dinner, and I returned home. Sunday nights, I watched college lectures from The Teaching Company. I had graduated with my Masters two months ago and held a crappy, entry-level job in my career field, but I had always liked college. Probably why I stayed for eight years. And probably why it took me eight years to do six years' amount of work. So I enjoyed listening to these lectures on DVD. Today's lecture was on the workers' rights movements of the early twentieth century.

Listening made me want to rebel.

Monday during my first break at work, I made a call to The Road Home, a group that worked with the homeless here in Salt Lake. I arranged a time for an interview so that I could start assisting in whatever way I could. My selfishness was sure to take many decades to overcome, so I knew I couldn't put off working on it any longer. I did want to be perfect one day.

When I got home, I dyed my hair red. Not auburn. Red. I wasn't a particularly interesting person, so I knew I had to work on that as well. And red hair was more interesting than mousy brown.

The next few weeks passed by uneventfully. Work was going okay, I was volunteering three hours a week at the soup kitchen, I finally started doing some yoga, and I was continuing to listen to my DVD lectures. Mom was visiting two Sundays a month, hardly complaining at all about my inadequate cooking. I was still hanging out with my former college classmates, and one day, Sarah issued me a challenge.

"You think you're so radical," she said, "but you're still a good little Mormon girl at heart."

"I never do my Visiting Teaching," I pointed out.

"Who does?" she returned.

"And I don't pay my tithing anymore."

"That just makes you a bad good little Mormon girl."

I frowned.

"Well, what's it to you?" I demanded.

"The Mormon Church is an oppressive power here in Utah. If you really believe all these liberal, intellectual ideals you say you do, then you have to take a stand."

"And just what do you propose?" I asked. "That I throw tomatoes at the temple?"

Sarah laughed. "Of course not, Pauline. I expect you to do something to *you*."

This puzzled me, and I continued frowning.

"You need to shave your head. Or get a nose piercing. Or get that tattoo you've been talking about for the past two years."

"And that'll lessen the power Mormons have?" I asked rebelliously. I hated how the Church treated gays. I hated how they treated women. I hated how even thirty-five years after blacks were finally allowed to hold the priesthood, they still had no stature in the Church.

Mostly, I hated that members were not allowed to think.

But other than write the occasional letter to the editor at the *Salt Lake Tribune*, I really didn't do very much.

"Any time you do *anything* that upsets the Mormons," insisted Sarah, "you're putting a crack in someone's defense."

"Are you sure I'm not just making them surround themselves with a thicker wall? Temple Square is already a compound. So is my mother's heart."

Sarah shrugged. "Your options are to do nothing or to do something."

"I dyed my hair red, didn't I?"

"Even old grandmas dye their hair red and purple and blue these days."

"Not Mormon grandmas."

The badgering continued another few minutes, and I eventually began to see Sarah's point. While I wasn't sure my getting a nose piercing would change the Prophet's mind about women holding the priesthood, I did think it was possible to get through *some* ideas to *some* Mormons. And some was better than none. On the other hand, I wasn't quite sure just what message my getting a tattoo would carry. Other than that it was okay to do things the Church disapproved of.

Maybe that was a good message.

And I truly had wanted a tattoo for many years now but had let the Church's teachings on body art scare me away. So the following Saturday, I went to a tattoo parlor I'd visited before with Sarah, and I explained what I wanted. The tattoo artist nodded, and we got started. It was a large design, on my back, and took three visits to complete. I slept on my stomach for quite a few days. Finally, a few weeks after everything had healed, I decided to show my mother the artwork when she came over one Sunday to visit.

"I have a surprise for you," I said cheerily, leading her to a chair in the kitchen.

"Oh, my heck, you're not pregnant, are you?" She put her hand to her head.

"Of course not, mother."

Now she put her hand on her chest in relief. "I'm sorry, Pauline, it's just that you're hanging out with homeless people now. Anything can happen."

"I donated to Al Franken, too."

"Oh, my heavens."

"And to Greenpeace."

"Oh, Pauline."

"And the Union of Concerned Scientists."

Mom put her hand up in the air like a stop sign and sighed heavily. "So what's the big surprise?" she asked. "You've started drinking and smoking? It was only a matter of time. Once you've begun your descent into the gutter, the outcome is pretty sure." She shook her head sadly.

"Mom, I've been drinking for six years."

"See what I mean?"

These conversations were always so irritating. I disapproved of Mormon missionary work, people going about telling everyone else they were wrong and we were right. So why was I doing the same thing with my mother?

"Okay, okay," I said. "Never mind. Let's eat our lunch." I put a nice Cobb salad on the table.

"No, no," said my mother. "You obviously want to tell me. Go ahead. I'm a big girl. I can take it. Did you have an abortion?"

"No, Mother. I use birth control. And I don't have herpes, either."

"Don't be vulgar, Pauline."

I wondered if it would be best to limit these Sunday luncheons to once a month. I rubbed my forehead and then decided to go ahead with what I'd planned. I was wearing a loose-fitting blouse and no bra, so I unbuttoned and turned my back on my mother to show her the tattoo.

"Oh, my God," she breathed.

I smiled, victorious at having gotten her to sin.

"What do you think?" I asked.

"Is that...is that the Plan of Salvation?" Mom asked timidly.

"You like it?" There was the Pre-Existence, the Veil, Earth, Paradise and Spirit Prison, and the three degrees of Glory.

"You left off Outer Darkness," Mom pointed out.

"There's room further down if I want to add it later," I said.

"On your…on your…" She pointed to my butt. "Oh, Pauline, putting Hell on your backside. It's just so…so…"

"Depraved?"

I pulled my shirt back on and buttoned up, taking several spoonfuls of salad onto my plate. Mom reluctantly followed suit, and we ate in silence for several minutes. Finally, she said softly, "I don't get it. If you wanted a tattoo, why did you get a *Mormon* tattoo?"

"I still believe."

At that, Mom started to cry. I sat there in silence, not knowing if I should continue eating or if I should put my hand on her arm. I ended up just sitting still for a couple of minutes and looking on uncomfortably.

"You okay, Mom?

She wiped at her eyes. "It's just that…that I expected you to become an alcoholic and drug addict and prostitute."

"I'm always open to suggestion," I said, smiling. Then I added, "There's a whole world out there, Mom, of perfectly happy people who aren't Mormon."

She shook her head. "I just don't understand."

I went to the refrigerator to take out a pitcher of lemonade and poured my mother a refill.

"So you'll keep rotating your food storage?" she asked weakly.

"Yes, Mom."

She nodded, and we ate another few minutes in silence. Then we each had a sugar cookie for dessert, and soon it was time for her to leave. We kissed at the doorway of my apartment, and Mom started out into the hall. After a couple of steps, she turned around.

"Get Outer Darkness added to your tattoo," she said firmly. "Men want all sorts of things. And use all sorts of language in private. Your boyfriends will need to be reminded of Satan's kingdom when they're doing you from behind."

My jaw dropped.

"Close your mouth, Pauline, before you swallow a fly." Mom smiled sweetly and started to turn away again but paused. "There are lots of things we need to talk about," she said carefully. "I think…I think I'm ready now. Perhaps we'd better up our Sunday visits from twice a month to every week. What do you think?"

I nodded silently, and Mom walked to the end of the hallway and started slowly down the stairs. I closed the door and headed for my sofa, where I picked up the phone and called Becky to set up a Visiting Teaching appointment.

# The God of Macramé

Dennis was afraid. Well, anyone would be afraid just minutes before going into surgery. He had to have six inches of his intestine removed. Even if the surgery were a success, it meant days of soreness and pain. And Dennis was such a wuss. He had passed out three times in his life after simply having blood drawn. Thank goodness the nurse had already inserted the IV. At least that ordeal was behind him. He hadn't even been able to watch. And thank goodness she'd gotten the vein on the first try. When he'd come in for an injection of dye, it had taken the nurse three attempts. Three! Dennis didn't know whether to start crying or to run out of the room.

It was all the more embarrassing because he was a sports writer for the Cincinnati newspaper. Here he was, a strong, virile man in his late forties, and he'd had nightmares about today's procedure for the past two weeks. What would happen if it got out that Dennis Merritt swooned at the sight of needles? It was something he didn't even tell his wife.

Last night, Dennis has asked his Home Teachers to come over and give him a priesthood blessing. It had absolutely infuriated him when Brother Stevens concluded with, "It shall be according to your faith." What kind of BS was that? Dennis wanted a blessing, not a test.

The pronouncement was all the more worrying because of the serious doubts he'd been having about Mormonism lately. He'd just secretly read two books, *By His Own Hand Upon Papyrus* by Charles Larson and *The Joseph Smith Egyptian Papyri* by Robert Ritner, and his faith was close to being shattered. The two books proved, beyond a doubt, that Joseph Smith had deliberately lied when claiming to translate the papyri he'd bought along with four mummies back in the 1830's. And if he lied about that, he obviously lied about translating the Book of Mormon. And if he lied about *that*, then there was no First Vision, no restoration of the priesthood, no prophecy, no nothing at all.

Those books were written by anti-Mormons, though. You could never trust an anti-Mormon. They were led by the Devil. It was all lies. Dennis was afraid to be without God. He wouldn't read such nonsense anymore. The Church was true. He knew it.

"Mr. Merritt," said a smiling young woman around thirty, coming into the room in her scrubs. "Are we all ready for our procedure?"

Was she being operated on, too?

"As ready as I'll ever be. Let's get this over with."

"You'll be in Recovery before you know it," she said with a bright smile.

Dennis smiled tightly back and closed his eyes as the nurse began rolling him into the hall. Dennis had sprained his ankle while riding his bike when he was about eight, and he'd had all four wisdom teeth pulled when he was twenty-five, but other than that, he'd led a healthy life. He was strong, fit, didn't even need Viagra. And now this. Was it a warning from God not to stray any farther? A punishment for having already strayed too far?

What kind of God loved his children and still tortured them for being human?

Soon Dennis was wheeled into the operating room and could feel the intensity of all the bright lights. Not heat, just intensity. He could hear murmuring and chattering about him but didn't focus on any of it. He wanted to be sure not to see a tunnel with a bright light in the distance. He wasn't ready to go just yet. His wife was an attractive woman. Dennis still enjoyed having sex with her. And he wanted to see his grandchildren. He wanted to watch more games. He wanted to cover the World Series. He wanted to cover the Super Bowl. He wanted to stop being afraid of needles.

He wanted time to regain his faith.

"Start counting backwards from one hundred," someone told him.

Dennis suddenly felt funny. They must have put something in the IV. He started counting backwards slowly. "100, 99, 98..." This was it. He was losing consciousness. He might never see his family again. He might be dying. He might be meeting Jesus.

He might be going to Outer Darkness.

After a moment, there was only blackness everywhere about him. But there was also a kind of peace, as if he no longer existed. He felt safe. Dennis wasn't sure how long he was out, but he suddenly felt a searing pain in his throat. He couldn't seem to open his eyes, so it took a few seconds to figure out what was happening. Someone was shoving a tube down his trachea. He couldn't breathe. He felt as if he were under three feet of snow after an avalanche, like that time at Snowbird. He was going to die. Oh, God.

Somehow, despite the continued feeling of suffocation, Dennis seemed to be getting oxygen. He started to calm down.

What was going on? This was so odd. He could hear talking and feel himself being touched. It was as if he were present and not present at the same time. It was like seeing the world through a veil. Like Earth life itself, only now he was aware of how difficult it was to see reality clearly under normal conditions. Only Heavenly Father could see everything with perfect clarity. Dennis understood that finally. It explained about the papyrus.

Dennis felt something cold and wet on his abdomen. What an odd sensation. It was like being bathed, only he could tell the liquid wasn't water. There was an alien quality to it. He wanted to ask what it was, but his mouth wouldn't work with that tube in it. And then he felt—a searing, terrible pain! Someone was cutting into him with a scalpel! He could feel it! Oh, God, the anesthesia wasn't working!

Dennis tried to scream but couldn't. He couldn't move his hands. He couldn't shake his head. He couldn't do anything at all. He was completely paralyzed. Oh, Heavenly Father, please! he prayed. Make them stop! Help me!

Dennis could feel skin being pulled back. He wondered if this was what it felt like to be scalped by Lamanites. Scalped! That must be where the word scalpel came from! Dennis could feel strange sensations inside his body. The pain was still intense but slightly less so. He tried to reach again for the tube in his throat. Maybe if he removed it, he could tell them all what was happening. His body felt like lead. Was this what it felt like to be mummified alive? He remembered all the horror movies he'd watched as a kid. The cruel things people did to appease their gods.

Dennis felt things being moved inside his abdomen. He felt clamps. Maybe he was imagining all this. Perhaps this was just another nightmare. God was punishing him by making this all seem so real. If you had to pinch yourself to tell if you were dreaming, was there any way to really know, if you couldn't move your fingers to pinch?

Perhaps this was what it felt like to be Isaac under the knife. Only God didn't stop the knife this time because Dennis didn't merit it.

Dennis deserved to die. He'd doubted. No, he'd actually stopped believing in the Church. It *was* all a lie. Oh, God, how could he live his life now when he'd wasted almost fifty years? His two oldest boys had already served successful missions in Japan and Argentina. His youngest was serving in Greece right now. They were spreading lies every day of their lives, just as Dennis had done back in Australia all those years ago.

Was it a sin to lie if you didn't know any better?

Was it a sin not to know better? This knowledge had been out there for decades.

If Dennis announced his conclusions, he'd be shunned by all his friends and relatives, treated like a leper, all in the name of God. Patricia might even demand a divorce. The kids might stop talking to him.

How did one start to live an authentic life at his age? When all he ever did was watch grown men play games?

Perhaps it had all been just a game for Joseph. And maybe it was all just a game to God as well. Dennis wondered what kind of Supreme Being would let so many of his children be deceived by so many different people. Isis hadn't been real. Zeus hadn't been real. Odin hadn't been real.

There was more searing pain. Dennis tried to scream again. When would this horrific misery end? He felt like a Jew in 1493 Spain. Please, God, let me die. Please, please. Help me. Help me. Dennis tried to go into a trance. He tried to meditate. But how could you meditate when your very insides were being cut out?

He thought of his promise in the temple to be disemboweled if he ever betrayed the Church. He heard someone say, "Clamp that bleeder."

Heavenly Father, I need you more than I've ever needed you before. Please, *please* help me. I need you *now*.

The pain continued unabated.

And that's when Dennis understood. In the Book of Abraham, Joseph Smith had written about the god of Mahmackrah. But that god was nowhere to be found in any other Egyptian or ancient literature anywhere.

Because there was no such god.

Might as well be the god of macramé.

There was clearly no Heavenly Father, either. It was *all* a lie. All of it. Not just the Mormon parts. Everything.

Odd how you could have a revelation when there was no god to deliver it.

"Okay, let's get this guy sewn up," said someone a few minutes later from somewhere in the blackness. Dennis felt needles piercing his skin. He felt thread pulling the flaps of his skin together. Several more minutes of misery passed. Then he felt the suffocating tube being pulled out of his throat. He almost gagged.

The needles had been nothing, he realized.

Then Dennis felt a light slap on the hand. A harder one on his face. "Wake up now," said a sweet, lilting voice. Dennis struggled to open his eyes. They felt so heavy.

He saw light.

"How are we feeling?" said the sweet, cheerful voice. He couldn't tell if it was the same nurse who'd brought him to the room or not. Probably not. The first nurse hadn't had time to scrub in.

It was amazing how clearly he could think.

"Like a new man," Dennis croaked. His throat was so sore.

The woman laughed. "Now that's the right attitude to have," she said, a smile clearly hidden behind her mask. "You're going to be just fine."

"Yes," he said slowly, lifting his hand and looking at his IV directly for the first time, his eyes narrowed. "Yes, I am."

# The Neurochemistry of Monday Night

Anita heard the car in the driveway and smiled. Don was home from work. That was always exciting, but especially on a Monday when they would soon have Family Home Evening. The weekly lesson and activity were even more of a highlight than Sunday at church. Anita enjoyed her interaction with the other sisters well enough, but church also required dressing up, always a challenge when you had a one-year-old daughter to wrestle with.

Little Melissa had turned one just two weeks ago. Anita had arranged a party for all her little friends from their Denver ward as well as a couple from the neighborhood. There had been a big cake to make, streamers to hang, ice cream to buy. She'd read *Clifford, the Big Red Dog* to all the little children, using her best voices. Anita knew that reading aloud to children increased the likelihood that they'd grow up to be regular readers themselves. The afternoon had been a celebration not only of her daughter's life, but for Anita, it was a confirmation that she'd made the right decision. Having met Don her senior year in college, she'd quickly fallen in love and converted to Mormonism. After finishing her Biochemistry degree, she'd been accepted to medical school but decided to marry in the temple instead and devote herself to being a wife and mother the way Heavenly Father intended.

It had taken about two years to get pregnant. Don had accused her once of secretly being on the pill, though a fertility test soon proved she wasn't the one lacking. Anita spent most of her time at the beginning of the marriage just learning how to cook. Don had made it quite clear he wasn't satisfied. Anita had been used to frozen dinners or a quick pizza. It had never been her life's goal to be a chef.

But tonight…Anita had prepared a Caesar salad, boiled some baby carrots in broth, fried some pork chops, made a quinoa dish with sliced sweet potatoes and chopped onions, and baked a coconut cake. Cooking was almost like chemistry class, when you thought of it, and that realization made it more bearable. Sunday was traditionally supposed to be the special meal of the week, but Anita preferred making Monday night special. Celebrating the family was celebrating one's very existence, one's whole purpose in life. She knew just when Don returned home every evening and timed finishing her meal tonight within two minutes of his driving into the garage.

"Hi, honey!" Anita called as she heard the door close. She turned the fire low on the pork chops and ran to greet him. She waited for him to put down his briefcase and take off his coat, and then she gave him a big hug and a kiss.

"Sheesh, give me a minute to breathe."

"Bad day?" Anita asked sympathetically.

"Every day's a bad day." He headed for the bedroom to change. Anita went back to the kitchen to finish the last bit of cooking and put everything on two bright yellow plates. She prepared a smaller plastic plate for Melissa and went to the living room to grab the girl out of her playpen and then insert her into a high chair. Melissa shouted happily.

"You know what's coming next, don't you?" Anita cooed.

Melissa giggled.

A few moments later, Don came into the kitchen and sat down in his chair heavily, staring at the plate in front of him. "I'm ravenous," he said, picking up his fork.

Anita liked when he used big words. She wanted their daughter to be educated, even if that didn't matter for Mormon women. But when Don scooped up a forkful of food, she raised her hand in protest. "The blessing!" she said.

Don frowned but put his fork down and offered a quick prayer on the food. Back in the early days he used to say, "Please bless the hands that prepared this," but lately he just got right down to the basics. "Thank you for this food. Please bless it that it will be good for us. We say this in the name of Jesus Christ. Amen."

He was clearly in a mood again. As his wife, it was Anita's job to make him feel better, tonight of all nights of the week. She had taken some courses about brain function in college but nothing really about psychology *per se*. She'd have to rely on the Spirit for guidance.

"How was your day, dear?" she asked as they began eating. After taking a mouthful herself, she helped Melissa with one. Half of it fell on the tray.

"They raised our goals. They're cutting overtime. They're cutting back on supplies. They're removing the cubicle walls so we can all see each other all the time."

Anita chewed for a moment. "Well, that'll be better than being isolated all day, won't it?"

"It's so they can check up on us more easily. Besides, they don't want us interacting. We'll be getting noise-canceling headphones to wear."

"Oh." She spooned another mouthful of quinoa into Melissa, wondering what to say next. The wife was supposed to stay at home not only to take care of the children and the house but also so she could stay untainted from the influence of the world. It was her purity that would keep her husband grounded. She was like a kidney or liver cleansing the body's fluids. She needed to get Don to think of something happy. Get his neurons rerouted. She turned to Don and added, "Anything *nice* happen today?" She had read something years ago about positive reinforcement.

"No."

They ate in silence for a couple of minutes, Melissa slapping the chair's tray happily so she could watch the tiny balls of fallen quinoa jump. Don seemed oblivious. Anita decided to tell him about her own day. "I bought some of the Atkins shakes for you to take to work," she said. She laughed. "You know, I think the grocery store tracks all my purchases and changes prices based on what I buy."

Don kept eating, making no sign he'd heard.

"I buy the Eas protein drinks for $5.49 for two weeks, and then they go up to $8.49. Then I buy the Atkins for $5.49 for two weeks instead, and then *they* go up to $8.49. If they see me buying anything on sale, they jack up the price."

"Uh-huh."

At least he was paying attention now. Anita talked about some of the good deals she'd managed to find at the grocery, including a great buy on some cleaning supplies. That led her to change direction in the conversation. "You know," she said, "I was cleaning the bathroom today, and you're really going to have to either start sitting down or aiming better."

"I'm not sitting down."

Ah, a complete sentence. She was getting somewhere. "Maybe we could take up archery on the weekends. Or golf. Something that requires aiming." She laughed. She was going to be positive.

How much of behavior was based on the physical wiring in the brain, Anita wondered. And how much on conditioning? And how did conditioning actually affect the physical wiring? Someday, she'd have to read up more on the subject.

Don served himself some more carrots in silence. Anita gave Melissa a carrot to chew on. It was wet and messy, but Melissa liked it.

"You should have seen what Melissa did today," said Anita, covering her smile with her hand since her mouth was half full. "She crawled from her swing to her playpen and stood up and shook the bars like she wanted to get *into* prison. Then she was happy there the rest of the day."

Don closed his eyes and ate another carrot.

"I played Lady Antebellum this afternoon, and Melissa tried to sing along with every song. It was so cute."

Anita looked at Don, who was now chewing the last bite of his pork chop. He still wasn't engaged. What was Anita doing wrong? She was being happy and cheerful and friendly. She was trying to distract her husband from his miserable day at work by helping him focus on his forever family. Why wasn't it working? Was she a bad wife?

She tried so hard to be a good Mormon, even when it meant giving up so much. Why wasn't God helping her do her job? It wasn't fair to ask her to sacrifice, and then make the sacrifice meaningless.

It wasn't really a sacrifice, of course. Anita loved being a wife and mother.

Well, maybe it *was* a sacrifice. She'd read somewhere that a sacrifice was giving up something good for something that was better.

Being a wife and mother was better.

She wondered briefly if she liked Monday nights because of its focus on the family, or if she liked the focus on the family because it made her believe for a few more days that she hadn't made the wrong decision. Was that how brain-washing worked? One made neural connections that were so strong they could resist interference from outside questioning.

Anita looked at Melissa. How could she ever consider Melissa a mistake?

Don was another matter. Anita tried to sprinkle her untainted influence on him, but he seemed to pour more tainted influence on her instead. Godliness had to be stronger than worldliness. If Anita wasn't getting through to him, she just wasn't trying hard enough.

Perhaps she should mention the lubricant she'd bought on sale today. Anita liked having sex on Monday nights, after all that attention on the family unit. It just seemed the appropriate way to cap the evening. And Don liked having sex any night Anita was in the mood. He even insisted on it some nights when she wasn't. It was her duty, after all.

She decided to go for it.

"I picked a new lubricant we can try," she said shyly. "It was forty cents cheaper than our usual brand, so I thought we could give it a shot."

At this, Don put down his fork and looked Anita in the face for the first time the entire meal. He sighed deeply and said, "God, you are so boring." Then he took a sip of his milk.

Anita stared at him in shock.

"I think sometimes I'd rather be at work slaving my life away than listening to you prattle on."

Anita felt her face burning. She turned to look at Melissa to make sure she hadn't understood. Melissa was smiling and trying to drink from her sippy cup.

Don stood up. "I'm going out with the guys tonight to watch football." He pushed his chair under the table. "Don't wait up." He grabbed his coat and was out the door in seconds, the car engine starting just a few moments after that. Anita sat staring at the empty space in front of her, her heart pounding. She stared for several minutes, until Melissa slapped the table and demanded another carrot.

Don hadn't even asked for any coconut cake.

"Well, of *course* I'm boring," Anita said aloud, picking out a carrot from the broth. "What choice do I have?"

Anita pretended the carrot was an airplane heading to Melissa's mouth. The girl giggled and grabbed it, half smashing it with her grip before shoving it into her mouth.

"Naturally, I love *you*," Anita cooed. "But where have *I* gone?"

She started cleaning up the table and washing dishes, leaving Melissa for last. Then she wiped the child down and carried her back to the playpen. She started to put her down on the soft cushion and then stopped in mid-air. Anita put the child on the rug instead.

"Haven't you been behind bars long enough?" she said. "Crawl around for a while."

Melissa looked up at her and smiled obliviously.

Anita sat on the sofa and watched the girl sitting happily, holding a stuffed bunny. So Don had left to get his neural receptors filled elsewhere. She could still have a special evening with her baby girl all by herself. She stood up and headed for her bedroom closet. "Don't get into any trouble while I'm gone," Anita called. Then she laughed, a little bitterly. "Well, it's okay to get into a *little* trouble." Anita rummaged in a couple of boxes at the back of the closet until she found what she was looking for. She pulled out an item and carried it back out to the living room, sitting again on the sofa.

"Introduction to Neurology," Anita announced. "We're going to start reading some big girl stories from now on." She opened the book, cleared her throat, and began reading.

# Group Sex for Faithful Mormons

I was never all that enticed by the idea of polygamy in the past. Maintaining four or five or six separate relationships seemed altogether too tiresome. Sex with Molly on Monday, Teresa on Tuesday, Wendy on Wednesday, and so forth. The idea seemed both too expensive and too regimented, even for someone like me who believed in authority. That all changed when I read Donna Banta's mystery novel *Seer Stone* and learned of another whole world of possibilities.

In that book, some faithful polygamists were debating whether or not a husband was obliged to have sex with his wives one at a time, or if he was entitled to have sex with all of them at once. The concept of morally acceptable group sex had never entered my mind as a viable possibility before.

But now...

Even though I'd been raised LDS, I sought out and joined a fundamentalist group that practiced polygamy. That didn't mean instant wives, of course. It took me a couple of years just to prove myself. Then, once I was deemed an acceptable saint, the courtship process was still supposed to happen over a number of years. No one married five wives all at once. You were supposed to court and marry one, then slowly solidify that relationship over the course of another year or so, then court and marry the second wife, and slowly solidify that relationship before moving on to number three, and so forth.

There was no way I was going to have enough patience for that. Such a lifestyle would still require years and years of the boring sex I wanted nothing to do with. So I broke tradition and courted five lovely young ladies all at the same time. Meredith was a vivacious twenty-two years old to my thirty. Roberta was twenty-one. Both Analisa and Catherine were eighteen. And Florence was the oldest at twenty-six. I balked a little at her age, but then she did have the biggest breasts of them all.

I have to admit, dating as a Mormon can be a bit frustrating. You're in it for the sex, but you can't actually have sex until you're married, and by then it's a little late to change your mind. It's quite a gamble, though our leaders liked to use the term "showing faith."

My own parents had plenty of sex, ending up with eight children. I was the youngest, and I can still remember hearing the screams and laughter coming from their bedroom as their headboard banged against the wall. They were certainly more than satisfied with one-on-one sex. I think it was something about the holidays that made me want more, though, when two or three of my married siblings could be heard through the walls of adjoining rooms having sex at the same time my parents were. So much sex at once quite titillated me as a young teenager. I can't remember the number of times I had to go to the bishop to confess my masturbation.

Or the number of times I went as a young adult. My masturbatory fantasies were exotic and wild, and I was chastised more than once by my various bishops.

But that was all over now. Tonight was my wedding night, and I'd share it with all five of my beautiful young brides.

The ceremony was nothing exceptional. It's not as if we had elaborate temples like the mainstream Mormons did. But our prophet married us himself, and then my women and I piled into my minivan and headed for the house I'd bought months earlier in anticipation of this very night. It sure helped that I had a good job, something uncommon for a polygamist. I think it was in part my tithing payments that allowed me to skip the normal courtship process and go straight for all five young women at the same time.

We walked into the house and all stood staring at each other nervously. While still a virgin myself, I realized I needed to be the leader here and set the tone. "Young ladies," I said, "we're going into the bedroom now and get more fully acquainted. I have a king-sized bed. We're all going to take off every piece of our clothing and enjoy ourselves the way Heavenly Father intended for married people to enjoy themselves."

There was a little nervous laughter, but most of the girls unfortunately seemed overly serious. I'd have to nip that in the bud. We walked into the bedroom, where I already had the lights set at just the right intensity. Too bright would dissuade people from letting go, and not bright enough would be far too frustrating. I wanted to see the tangle of bodies surrounding me.

I undressed and lay on the bed with my staff pointing toward the ceiling. Only Meredith had fully disrobed by this time, and she stood beside the bed, unwilling to climb on. Soon Roberta and Catherine were also naked, and finally Analisa and Florence were ready as well. Two stood to the right of the bed, two to the left, and one at the foot. I surveyed them all in their magnificent youthful beauty and smiled.

Afraid the girls would be too hesitant to engage fully, I decided to give some directions. "You," I said, pointing at Analisa, "are going to get behind me and lick my asshole." Her eyes widened. "While you," I said, pointing at Catherine, "are going to start sucking my dick." She smiled weakly. "And you,"

I said, pointing now at Florence, "are going to rub your breasts in my face." She nodded submissively. "And you other two are going to join in however you can. Maybe suck my toes or something." I looked each one in the face and grinned. "Now let's get the party started!" I got to my knees on the bed and nodded for everyone to begin following directions.

Soon the first three players were in position, and I was luxuriating in the feel of stimulation from a variety of angles. This was everything I'd hoped it would be. Soon I'd have them all laid out in a row, and I'd shove my dick into each one for ten seconds each, playing a kind of musical chairs until the lucky one got a load of cum in her twat. The possibility of variations we could experience every evening had me harder than I'd ever been in my life.

Suddenly, there was the sound of a long-winded foghorn.

I looked about in confusion, and Florence started laughing. "What was that?" I asked.

Florence was pointing at Analisa, who even in the dim light was clearly flushed.

"I'm sorry," Analisa whispered. "I…I get flatulent when I'm nervous."

At this, Roberta started giggling uncontrollably. She kept it up for a full thirty seconds as I stared at the girls in astonishment. Meredith had her arms crossed over her chest, trying to kiss me while still keeping her guard. When I slapped the mattress in frustration, Catherine said, "I'm feeling dizzy." She put her hands to her head. "I always pass out if I get too nervous." That said, she fell right onto the floor in a heap. Roberta giggled even harder, sounding like a hyena. Meredith was trying to ignore the chaos, kneeling in front of me now, her arms still crossed over her chest like a Venus de Milo in a straightjacket, as she bobbed back and forth over my dick. Analisa tooted again.

Florence inserted one of her nipples into Analisa's mouth, and I slapped the mattress again. "Hey, no lesbianism here! I want all your attention focused on me! Give *me* that nipple!"

I tried to get the situation back under control, ordering Analisa to suck on my balls while Meredith continued to deal with my dick. Then I had Roberta squat over my face so I could lick her labia.

"What the hell!" I shouted, spluttering.

"I'm so sorry," said Roberta, giggling again. "I also pee a little when I get nervous."

"Look," I said, trying to remain calm. "I'm your husband, your lord. This is all ordained by God. Your whole purpose is to satisfy me, especially tonight. Now, let's get ourselves in gear." I pointed at Meredith, about to give her an order, when suddenly, I felt an excruciating pain and yelled.

"Sorry," mumbled Analisa. "I was just trying to improvise."

"Well, stick your finger up your own ass and try to stop that whistle-blowing, but leave *my* asshole out of this."

"You wanted me to lick it earlier."

"Are you *arguing* with me?" I took a deep breath and tried to calm down. "All right," I said, "everyone lay down next to each other."

"What about Catherine?" said Florence. "She's still on the floor."

"All right, everyone on the floor. Her hole works just as well while she's unconscious. Spread her legs a little for me."

The four remaining girls complied, and I shoved my dick into Roberta first. I slid in and out for several seconds and then moved on to Catherine for several more, and then moved on to Analisa. As I entered her, we all heard another foghorn blast. The smell was overpowering.

"Sorry."

"Look," said Florence, "let us each go down on you for a while. That's easy enough, and it'll calm us all a bit." She pushed me on my back and opened her mouth, enveloping me instantly.

"Teeth! Teeth!" I shouted.

"Sorry."

I heard another toot nearby, and Roberta giggling uncontrollably.

I smelled urine.

"I'm starting to get nauseated," said Florence, putting her hand to her mouth. She heaved, and I dodged out of the way just in time. Most of it landed in Analisa's hair. This caused her to heave onto Catherine, still on the floor. This in turn sent Roberta scrambling for the bathroom, though she didn't quite make it in time. Meredith opened a window and screamed.

I won't go into every horrifying detail of that interminable evening. Suffice it to say that the next day, I demanded an annulment of all five marriages. I put my house on the market and headed back for Salt Lake. I'd marry just one girl in the temple, and if that didn't satisfy me, I'd just have to try an affair or two. Heavenly Father would understand, had perhaps made these decisions himself on his way to godhood. An affair would only be with one woman at a time, but maybe after I had a little experience with several different women separately, I could try something like this again.

How did God the Father handle this up in heaven now, I wondered, with perhaps hundreds or even thousands of wives? He must really be quite the man. I found myself more impressed with him now than I had been before when I thought of him only as the Creator of planets and stars. He really was a guy worth following.

Sitting in church, I'd watch the other couples come in, one man and one woman, and sigh. Maybe monogamy was simply the price we had to pay before we could become gods and have group sex throughout the ages.

Even masturbation lost some of its appeal over the next few months. I always kept smelling urine and methane whenever I came. I tried watching erotic movies, but nothing really quite worked for me. I ended up beginning to write Mormon porn stories under a pseudonym. There was a surprisingly large audience for them.

But even as I started dating again, life simply seemed less exciting these days. What if sex, with one woman or even ten, just wasn't what it was cracked up to be? Life itself seemed meaningless under such circumstances, much less eternity.

I went to work every day, went to church on Sunday, and every Sunday evening sat down to write a story and then beat off. In my daydreams, I came between women's legs, in their mouths, in their faces, on their breasts, on their backs. I'd lie in bed afterward, dreaming about that hot receptionist at work who I might ask out, and the wife of the Elders Quorum president who I might win away from him. I made sure to pay my tithing and do my home teaching. I was going to make it to the Celestial Kingdom and have Celestial sex for the rest of forever.

I laughed when I heard Christians from other faiths talk about how Jesus was celibate. He was up there banging away at forty women right at this moment.

I wrote a letter to Church headquarters, asking if one of the apostles could address the topic of eternal sex in General Conference, but so far, they haven't said anything. Still, I already know enough.

Women in the mainstream Mormon Church didn't seem to like me as well as those in the fundamentalist sect, but I kept asking them out. They kept turning me down, but that only meant when I did get them in the next world, I'd just be a little more demanding.

As another celibate year passed, I began considering returning to the polygamous group. Even a little urine and methane was better than living like this, I thought. I finally did return, but because of my earlier defection, I was required to serve faithfully three more years before I was allowed to start courting again. Of course, by this time, all five of my former wives had long since married other men, and because so many other men had taken multiple wives, there weren't many available girls left to choose from.

I tried courting two eighteen-year-old sisters, but they ended up being snatched away by a younger man who was more in favor with the prophet.

Then finally, one day it happened. There was an underground group of older men who'd been denied wives who took to having sex with each other, and I was initiated into that group. None of us was gay, but it was infuriating knowing other men in our community were getting what they wanted every night and we were getting nothing. We really had no choice. Men came in my face and on my chest and in my ass. I sucked dick and licked assholes and bit nipples. I was told what to do and how to do it. I stuck my tongue in hairy ears and licked calloused toes. A couple of the men had hygiene problems, but I learned to accept the taste of head cheese.

And despite finally being able to have sex regularly after all those years, it just wasn't very fulfilling. But maybe this is what we had to do for now in order to earn good sex for eternity.

I'd do anything for good sex.

I started writing fundamentalist Mormon porn. There was actually quite an audience for that as well.

I went to work, went to church, got fucked by ugly old men, wrote stories, and beat off.

One day, I told myself every evening, I'd be a god. Things would be different when I was a god.

Then I'd sigh, take a long shower, and go meet the group for sex.

# The Bishop's Husband

It was Saturday. Date Night. And it was now 8:29 in the evening. Thayne looked at his watch and sighed. *As Time Goes By* had just ended on PBS. Date Night was the one day a week Thayne and Gareth cooked a special meal as a couple. The one night a week they sat down to watch a movie together. Thayne had suggested chicken for tonight, and Gareth had agreed to pick up some free-range breasts at Safeway on his way home after stopping at the Hall in the late afternoon.

Thayne thought about how Gareth had joined the Freedom Socialist Party only a little over a year ago and had already been voted onto the Executive Committee. He had Exec meetings regularly, routine Hall meetings, Study Group, newspaper sales, and Spanish class. Plus the extra assignments of cooking meals for evening forums, making signs, doing bookkeeping, mailings, and other assorted chores. He was at the Hall almost every day. Most of the time, Thayne didn't mind.

Gareth had joked that he felt as if he were back at church. Both Thayne and Gareth had grown up Mormon and were used to holding two or three or four "callings" at one time, spending half their free time with other church members. Thayne had heard Gareth comment more than once that the camaraderie he felt at the Hall was the closest thing he'd ever found to what they'd both experienced at church before being excommunicated and losing 99% of their friends in one fell swoop ten years ago. Thayne envied Gareth's new circle of friends, but he didn't want to become a Socialist. Those guys talked about overthrowing the government. It was all talk, of course. They'd never do anything more radical than hold a protest, and there were only a handful of members in any event, but the rhetoric made Thayne uncomfortable.

It was 8:45. Gareth had called at 6:30 to say he was running late. He'd called again at 7:30 to say he was about ready to leave. Thayne grabbed the phone and dialed.

"I'm on my way now, honey," Gareth said as he picked up his cell.

"Okay," Thayne replied and hung up. He didn't say good-bye. He was too annoyed.

Five minutes later, the phone rang. Was Gareth calling to question Thayne's rudeness?

"Have you eaten? Shall I pick up some chicken at Ezell's?"

"I was waiting for dinner with you."

"I'll get some chicken. Sorry, honey."

Thayne opened a can of baked beans, poured the contents into two bowls, and heated them in the microwave. Once they were steaming hot, he set them on the coffee table where he and Gareth usually ate. Then he set out two cans of Safeway diet orange soda and two empty blue ceramic plates. He put the chipped plate where Gareth would be sitting. Then, thinking about it a moment, he put the chipped plate where he would be sitting himself.

Then he put it back at Gareth's place.

It was just after 9:00. Thayne went to sit outside on the porch in his bare feet. Gareth pulled up to the house at 9:10.

9:10. Thayne was so irritated. The two men had been together for a decade, and early on in the relationship, Thayne had started greeting Gareth when he came home with a wild, energetic wave of his hand as if he were a little child. Gareth always smiled when he saw the wave. Thayne didn't feel like waving tonight, but he forced himself to do it.

Gareth grinned as he walked up the front steps carrying a huge, white cardboard box filled with chicken. They kissed, and Thayne took the box and set it on the coffee table.

"How was your day?" asked Thayne. He had a regular 9 to 5 weekday job, but Gareth worked seven days a week as a painter.

"Almost finished the house in Northgate. Boy, was it hot this afternoon. Radio said it was another record high. Then I got to the Hall around 4:30."

"You've been in Spanish class since 4:30?"

Gareth laughed. "No, if it was Spanish class, I'd have just left. We were getting ready for the rally tomorrow."

There was going to be a rally to protest political inaction over climate change at Westlake in downtown Seattle the next afternoon. It would be coordinated with rallies across the nation and even around the world, people protesting in over 160 countries.

"It took four hours to make signs?" asked Thayne, hoping he didn't sound as petulant as he felt. "How many people from the Hall are we expecting to come?" He deliberately tried to use inclusive words when he talked about the Hall, even though Gareth was quite aware of Thayne's feelings toward the Party.

No sense emphasizing how far apart they'd grown over the past year or so.

A news story from a few years back, about the break-up of the relationship between Susan Sarandon and Tim Robbins, flashed through Thayne's mind. They'd seemed the perfect Hollywood couple, but Sarandon said they'd simply drifted apart over the years. Thayne had heard many couples say that. Now he was seeing what it actually meant.

He'd wanted his relationship with Gareth to last forever, just as if they'd been married in the temple.

"Hopefully, all of them will come," said Gareth. "But it wasn't just signs. I had to make up a flyer, too."

Thayne put a breast and a thigh on Gareth's plate, along with two rolls. He skipped the rolls himself, needing to lose a few pounds, but put another breast on his plate. Gareth went to the kitchen to get butter to put on his roll. Thayne started pulling the skin off his breast.

"How was *your* day?" asked Gareth, returning to the sofa.

"I read a hundred pages of my book." Thayne was reading *This Changes Everything* by Naomi Klein, about how Capitalism would never allow the cooperation necessary for countries around the world to work together in the fight against climate change. There would have to be a massive redistribution of wealth. Rich people and corporations were going to fight the idea, but humans were simply going to have to make the ideological shift, or they were going to face a catastrophe so tremendous that while they might survive as a species, they wouldn't survive as a civilization. It made Thayne think that perhaps Socialism was the way to go, after all. The folks down at the Hall seemed like fringe elements of society, all of them quirky and odd, but when Thayne watched Naomi on *Bill Moyers*, she looked and sounded like a calm, reasonable, normal person.

"Uh-huh."

"I took a long walk, I listened to music, I took a nap, and I emailed some friends."

"Sounds like you had a good day."

Thayne chewed his chicken silently for a moment. "You know," he said slowly, "I really enjoy my time alone."

"I know you do."

"But I don't like spending *all* my time alone. I want to see you sometimes, too."

"Sorry I got home so late."

Thayne ate another bite in silence. He didn't know if making a fuss would be helpful or hurtful. He didn't want to make things any worse than they already were. And he didn't want to be the nagging spouse. Gareth was doing a lot of important things. He wanted to be supportive. He kept eating in silence.

"You okay, Thayne?"

Thayne took a swig of his orange soda and turned to Gareth. "I feel like the bishop's wife," he said calmly. "You're always at the church."

Gareth looked shocked and hurt at the same time, a piece of chicken halfway to his mouth as he stopped in horror at the words. He hated any comparison with how he lived his life now with how Mormons lived their lives. "That's—that's not fair," he finally managed.

"I understand you have an obligation to the world," said Thayne. "And an obligation to your friends. But you have an obligation to me, too."

There. He'd said the dreaded word. Obligation. Hardly a romantic notion. If Gareth were just spending time with him out of a sense of obligation, the relationship was already over.

"I miss you," said Thayne. "I understand if you're busy four or five other nights of the week. But you have to dedicate at least one night to me. Tonight is Date Night. And you weren't here."

"Well, it was an emergency. There's that rally tomorrow."

"Gareth, you guys have known about that rally for weeks. There's been plenty of time to make signs and write flyers."

Gareth stared at his thigh, while Thayne tore a hard to get piece off the leg he was now working on.

"You could always come down and help," said Gareth in a small voice.

"There's a reason the bishop's wife doesn't get called to be Relief Society president at the same time her husband is the bishop."

"Stop using all these Church references!"

"And there's a reason Monday night is always reserved for family, no matter what other obligations a person may have."

There was that damn word again.

Thayne carried his plate to the kitchen, dropped the chicken bones into the compost pail, and washed his plate. Even tomorrow, the rally wouldn't exactly be a time they could "share." Gareth had to leave the house three hours early so he could first meet with a sponsee from AA. Thayne thought about how he'd stayed with Gareth through his alcoholism and recovery, both difficult times. But then, Gareth had stayed with Thayne after Thayne was diagnosed with genital herpes after making one very bad decision when Gareth was hitting rock bottom. After meeting with his sponsee in the morning, Gareth would then have to go to the Hall, get the signs and flyers, and drive down to Westlake to help set up. Thayne would have to take public transportation to get there. Even once Thayne arrived, the crowd would probably be too big for him to reach Gareth.

The family that protests together…

Thayne walked back out to the living room and sat down on the sofa again. "Do…do you want to watch a movie tonight?" asked Gareth.

"It's 9:30," said Thayne. "You know I go to bed at 10:00."

"Well, can't *you* make some concessions? It's not all about *me* compromising, is it?"

"I already compromise by accepting that you work every weekend, when you don't have to. We already only have a few hours together at best. And now you're taking even that away from me."

There was silence for a couple of moments. Gareth was holding a piece of chicken but not eating it. Thayne felt like a heel for making him unhappy. Was that what couples did? If Gareth made Thayne unhappy, did Thayne have to turn around and make him unhappy as well?

A marriage made in heaven.

"Gareth," said Thayne softly, "I understand if I'm not your top priority. But I can't stay with you if I'm not *somewhere* on your list of priorities. Can you understand that?"

"I just want to make the world a better place."

Thayne thought for a moment. What Gareth said reminded him of some AA saying Gareth had told him at some point. "Didn't you once tell me that you need to keep your own side of the street clean?"

"Yes?"

"Family *has* to come first. If you can't create happiness and justice at home, you're not going to be able to do it anywhere else, either."

"You're just David O. McKay incarnate, aren't you?" Gareth forced a little smile.

"Maybe the Mormons have *some* things right."

"Like having the bishop spend three hours at the church every evening?"

"Every evening except one."

Gareth carried his plate to the kitchen and then came back to pack up the remaining pieces of chicken and place them in the refrigerator. He was in the kitchen a long while, and then he slowly walked back out to the living room. "You know Café Vignole?" he asked, wiping off the coffee table.

"The place just down the hill. Yes?"

"They're open till twelve."

"Okay."

"If you can stay up a little late tonight, I'll take you down there and we can have coffee and talk till midnight."

Thayne thought for a moment.

"Thayne?"

"Can I suck you off in the truck afterward?"

Gareth laughed. "You are so demanding. But that's why I love you."

"I love you, too, you know."

"I'll work just six days a week from now on. *All* day Saturday will be yours."

"Thank you." Thayne grabbed Gareth's hand and held it tightly.

Gareth leaned over and kissed Thayne on the lips. "Let me just go wash my dick and we can go."

Gareth headed for the bathroom, and Thayne started singing. "There is beauty all around...when there's love at home..."

"I'm gonna slug you," came out muffled through the bathroom door.

Thayne smiled and sat down to put on his shoes.

# Also by Johnny Townsend

Mormon Underwear

God's Gargoyles

The Circumcision of God

Sex among the Saints

Zombies for Jesus

Mormon Fairy Tales

Flying over Babel

Dinosaur Perversions

The Gay Mormon Quilter's Club

The Abominable Gayman

Marginal Mormons

Mormon Bullies

The Golem of Rabbi Loew

The Mormon Victorian Society

Dragons of the Book of Mormon

Selling the City of Enoch

A Day at the Temple

Gayrabian Nights

Let the Faggots Burn: The UpStairs Lounge Fire

Latter-Gay Saints: An Anthology of Gay Mormon Fiction (co-editor)

Available from BookLocker.com or from your favorite neighborhood or online bookstore.

Follow Johnny on his blog, QueerMormon.com, or on Twitter @QueerMormon

CPSIA information can be obtained
at www.ICGtesting.com
Printed in the USA
FSOW01n1524041114
3385FS

9 781632 634832